EVIL AND EVERGLADES

Published by Airplane Books

A Kip Yardley Mystery
©2012 By Don Yarber

ISBN-10:
098506952X
ISBN-13:
978-0-9850695-2-0

Evil and Everglades

Don Yarber

This book is dedicated to the memory of:

David Holt, a good friend and a good golfer. Rest in peace, my friend

Prologue:

The Florida sun had just peeked its gleaming head over the calm waters of Biscayne Bay and the Atlantic when Tami Fawn left the house for her daily run along the narrow beach path. She felt vibrant and alive. The evening before this beautiful day, her mother, Mona Fawn, had discovered that she held a ticket with all the winning numbers in the Florida Power Vault lotto; the ticket was worth $114 million.

Tami had just met a friendly private detective from LA that she really liked. The three of them had celebrated until nearly 1 a.m. It was only 5:30 but Tami was exuberant, alive with excitement, and enjoying the cool morning air as she knelt in the sand and performed stretching exercises in preparation for her morning run.

When she stood up she looked ahead and saw strange marks in the sand, not thirty feet from where she stood. At first glance it looked as if a sea turtle had clawed its way from the water towards the saw grass and palmettos, ten yards from the water's edge.

She walked to the spot and knelt. Upon closer examination she realized that it hadn't been a turtle that made the marks. Something had been dragged through the sand. A brown blotch of sand stretched in nearly a straight line towards the palmettos. Frightened, she realized that the blotch looked like blood. Maybe a gator had nabbed a manatee and was at this moment enjoying its breakfast.

She walked toward the saw grass, following the drag marks. She weaved her way around the spreading branches of a mangold tree and suddenly there was a body right in front of her in the sand.

It was a female, dressed in denim shorts and a tee shirt with the words "I'm a Homesteader" in black letters. Tami let out a stifled cry. The tee shirt was a Christmas present from her to Mona.

She stepped closer. It was her mother. Mona's throat had been cut from ear to ear. A pinkish, gaping flesh wound exposed dangling arteries, part of the windpipe, and a lot of blood.

She screamed.

CHAPTER ONE

It was hot in Miami when I drove south through the city. I had the top up on my Austin Healey and the aftermarket air conditioner was running full force, but the heat was suffocating.

I had been awakened by a phone call from Dade County Central Hospital. They asked if I knew a Tami Fawn. I answered yes, although I really had only met Tami the previous day.

The previous day was my first day in the Miami area on a vacation that was long overdue.

* * * * * * * * * * * * * * * * *

I had driven south out of Miami and was walking the beach, near a private development of million dollar homes near Key Largo. Tami Fawn was sunbathing in a bikini that was both provocative and revealing, yet modest compared to some of the thong type bikinis worn by other women on the beach.

Her body was tanned but I could tell that was her natural complexion. She was not more than five feet two inches tall and in the neighborhood of 120 pounds. She had the kind of body that God must have had in mind when he placed Eve in the Garden of Eden.

Her hair was long and black, the kind of black you see when you close your eyes tightly in the middle of the night. It was wavy in the right places, and shiny as a piece of polished black coral.

Her lips were small and pouting the color of clouds dyed red by the setting sun. She wore no lipstick. Her lips were the kind that didn't need it.

My gaze wandered from her face, branched out on her arms and then down across perfect small breasts, over her tight tummy and down the kind of legs photographed most for Victoria's Secret catalogs.

When I walked by, she rose up on one elbow, looked at me and smiled. I smiled back.

"Hello," she said.

"Good morning," I murmured.

"Beautiful day isn't it?" she asked.

"Couldn't be better," I said, not knowing what else to say.

I am not a young man. There was a time when I would have jumped ten feet straight up to be talking to a girl like this. But time changes things.

I am Kip Yardley, past sixty, and getting over a relationship that has haunted me for the past month or so. Back in LA I have a fairly successful private investigating firm. A case in the south Pacific had been finished a few months back and I had made a quarter of a million dollars. I used the money to expand my office, hire a secretary, employ some associate investigators and buy the Austin Healey, a car I had dreamed of forever.

But the one thing that money cannot buy (other than health) is happiness. I had been involved in a relationship with Rhonda, a beautiful girl much younger than me. Rhonda had tiptoed around the "M" word many times. After my windfall case, she finished tiptoeing and started stomping around it. Marriage was the furthest thing from my mind.

She had never been married. I was long since divorced. She didn't have children. I had four, all grown. She wanted to get married, settle down, have kids, and go to PTA meetings. The only meetings I wanted to go to were when the Dodgers met the Mets or the Lakers met the 76'rs. And an occasional family reunion.

So things went sour.

I needed to get away from California for a while, forget about Rhonda, and free my mind and spirit. I don't know why I had chosen to vacation in Florida. California offers everything that Florida has, and then some. I think it was the yearning for something new, a desire to get something going in my life. It might have been a running away, or a desire to forget. My love life was in a shambles. Rhonda had been a constant companion for more than five years, now that part of my life was fading away fast.

Tami Fawn continued the conversation by making small talk about the weather, about the color of the sand, the way the sunlight glistened on the water and a lot of other things, most of which I can't remember. We sat side by side, me in shorts and a tee shirt, Tami in her bikini. I introduced myself as Kip. She told me her name was Tami.

I wondered how far a relationship might go with Tami. Of course the male instinct in me was thinking of things other than PTA meetings. I kept up my end of the conversation by agreeing with whatever she was saying.

"Do you come here often?" I asked, a line as old as the story of the woman at the well.

"I work near here, at the hospital," she said. "I come here sometimes after work just to relax and catch some sun. My car is in the shop so I took the bus to work. Buses are so slow."

I agreed with her and remained silent for a long time, not knowing what to say.

"Isn't it funny how the fattest women wear the skimpiest bikinis?" she asked, laughing.

"Yep." I answered.

"You don't talk much, do you?" she finally blurted out.

"It surprises me that you are talking to me." I said, honestly.

"Why?" she asked.

"I'm probably twice your age, I'm a stranger, and I'm thinking how much I'd like to take you to dinner tonight."

"Don't be silly," she said, laughing. "You are a man, I'm a woman. It's natural that we should be talking to one another, according to Mona."

"Who's Mona?" I asked.

"She's my Mom," Tami said, smiling. "The smartest woman on earth."

"If she said we should be talking to one another, I would have to agree with that statement." I said.

Tami laughed again, a full-hearted laugh that came from a place where only truth and sincerity live.

"What do you do, Kip?" she asked.

"I am a lecher. I chase young women," I said, putting on a false sneer.

She laughed again.

"That probably doesn't pay much," she said. "Are you retired?"

I was momentarily set back by her stab at my manhood, but soon realized that she only meant it as a joke, not a personal attack on my libido.

"I'm a private detective from LA." I said.

"I'm Tami Fawn," she said, smiling. "I'm a nurse at Dade County Center Hospital." She pointed in a direction north and west. I could see a large building complex stretching towards the city of Miami.

I extended my hand and she placed her small bronze hand in mine.

"I'm very pleased to meet you, Tami Fawn," I said. "Kip Yardley, displaced PI, at your service."

"So you're not retired?" she asked.

"No, not yet," I said. "I've got a few good years left in me, and I enjoy my work. I'm just here on vacation, trying to get my life back together after a relationship."

"I understand," she said, suddenly solemn. "Relationships are like luxury cruises, you feel good when you are on them but when they end you have a let down."

"I've never heard it put that way," I said, "but that's a good analogy."

"Do you catch the bad guys?" she asked, grinning. "Or is that all on TV?"

"I've caught a few," I admitted. "But you are right, that's mostly on TV. The big cases are few and far between. I just finished a good one though. And I caught the bad guys. I enjoy my work."

We were silent for a few seconds. I glanced at the ocean, then at my watch. My hands were starting to tremble as they had in the past when I knew I was getting close to a woman.

"So how about dinner?" I asked.

"Oh, sorry," she said. "I can't. I promised Mom I would help her write some letters tonight."

"Maybe you could call her and postpone it. Or maybe she can write them without you," I said.

"You don't understand," she said. "Mom doesn't know how to write. She doesn't know how to read very well. Besides, I promised. I try never to break a promise I make to my mom."

"Well that's commendable," I said. "Can I call you and set up a date for another time?" My hands were still trembling slightly.

"I've got an idea," she said. "Maybe you could take me home, meet Mom, and have dinner with us?"

"Shouldn't you phone your mom and ask her first?"

"She won't care, Kip," she said. "What do you say? I know she'd like to meet you."

I was silent for a moment. It occurred to me that a girl who wants me to meet her mother might also want to talk about the "M" word. I didn't need that in my life at this point. That was the reason for the last relationship's demise.

"No strings?" I asked.

"Meaning?"

"I mean that most young ladies who invite guys to meet their moms have ulterior motives. You know, come home and let me introduce you to my family before we get serious."

"You are presumptuous aren't you?" she asked, not smiling.

"I'm sorry," I said, and meant it. "It's just that I'm not ready for a commitment and I was assuming that meeting a girls parents was part of that general idea."

"OK," she said. "Forget it. I was just being friendly."

She stood up and picked up her beach mat as if to go.

"Wait," I said. "I'm sorry. I'd love to meet your mom. And that was presumptuous of me, and rude. Please, forgive me and lets start over, OK?"

She stood there looking down at me for a long minute.

"You'll like my mom," she said, smiling again. "She's about your age."

I wasn't sure how to take that.

"So, Mr. Kip Yardley," she said. "If you want to give me a ride home it will save me the trouble of waiting for public transportation."

I gave her a ride.

CHAPTER TWO

I drove as Tami talked. She had been born and raised near Homestead. The town had derived its name from a railroad engineer. When the railroad was being built south to the Keys the town didn't have a name, it was just a spot where people were starting to homestead land. Eventually an engineer marked a spot on a map as "Homestead" and thus a town was born.

She told me that her mother had become pregnant while still in school, enticed by an older man. The man ran away and joined the army and she had never known him. Her mother had then met Joshua Hayden, one of the railroad workers, and Josh had been the only father she had ever known. He had died late last fall after a long battle with cancer.

I murmured my condolences and she shrugged them off.

"God gave Joshua to my mom and me to be part of our lives. He had the right to take him away from us. And honestly, Josh is in a better place, a place where there is no pain."

I was astounded at her simplicity. I was also acutely aware of the fact that I wanted desperately to kiss and caress this child of faith. Flesh hungers for flesh. I am a man first, a believer second. Not the way it should be, but the way it is. God hates a hypocrite.

She went on to say that she had graduated from Dade County High School and got her nursing degree at Homestead College. She was 31 years of age and had not been married. An engagement had ended in the tragic death of her fiancé in the Iraqi War. She liked men and enjoyed their company. Since the death of her fiancé she had been attracted to two men, neither relationship had lasted. Her philosophy was to help the sick through her nursing career and to enjoy life and take one day at a time, and to see what the future might hold.

She admired the Austin Healey and asked if she might drive it sometime. I said "sure" and started to pull off of the road to let her take the wheel.

"Not now," she said, "maybe sometime."

By the time we got to her home it was after six. The house was a typical south Florida dwelling, concrete block that had been stucco covered, an attached carport, a screened in lanai. It wasn't big, five rooms and one bath, and set a quarter of a mile off of the main drag in a sandy area surrounded by palmettos. It was a hundred yards away from the beach. Tami told me that her mother owned the two hundred acres surrounding the home and that the price of real estate had gone up in the surrounding area.

"Mom has threatened to sell more than once," she said. "I keep urging her not to sell, but since Josh died, we've been on the verge of poverty a few times trying to pay off his hospital bills. Mona is tired of always trying to make ends meet, my meager salary helps, but by the time we pay hospital bills, insurance and utilities, the rest is set aside for groceries and household needs. There isn't much left. Mom's grandfather offers to help, but Mona is very stubborn about that."

I was intrigued by the way she referred to her mother as "mom" in one sentence and used her proper name "Mona" in the next. I've known people from the south who have never called their parents "mom" or "dad" but "Mary" and "Tom" or whatever their proper names happened to be.

Must be a "Southern Thing", I told myself.

I parked the Healey in a spot that she indicated and we walked to the house. She opened the unlocked door and went in ahead of me.

"Mom, we've got company," she called out.

"Come in, whoever you are," I heard a voice say. The voice was light and feminine and I recognized the similarity between it and Tami's voice right away.

"Come out and meet my new friend, Mom," Tami said.

"Be right out, Hon," the voice said. "I'm finishing the dishes before I start supper."

I waited. Tami motioned at a well-worn couch, blue floral pattern, with high back and rolled arms. I sat down and almost immediately had to stand as Mona Fawn entered the room. She was nearly a spitting image of her daughter, Tami. A few wrinkles around her eyes and across her brow were the obvious differences.

"Hello," she said, smiling.

"How do you do?" I said, waiting for an introduction. Tami had already walked through the living room and down a hallway, out of sight.

"I'm Kip Yardley," I said, extending my hand.

She took my hand and pumped it like a farmer's wife might have pumped water, lifting it high and dropping it low.

"My name is Mona," she said. "I'm Tami's mom."

She spoke with just the smallest trace of a lisp. I would have guessed her age at not more than 40.

"Pleased to meet ya." she said. I detected the southern drawl.

"It's nice to meet you, Ma'am." I said.

She looked me over good, her eyes roamed from the top of my nearly six-foot frame down to the beach flip-flops I was wearing on my feet.

"You are tall," she said, smiling.

"Not really," I said. "I'm just a shade under six foot."

"Excuse me, Kip," she said, dropping my hand. "I am starting supper. Will you stay and eat with us?"

"Thank you," I said, "That's very nice of you to ask."

"Not often we get a good looking man to have supper with us, Kip," she said.

It embarrassed me and I remained silent. The silence was broken when Tami came back in the room. She had changed from her bikini and robe to a pair of jeans with a tee shirt that said "Nurses Do It With Compassion" across its front.

"I see you two have met," she said.

"Yes," I answered.

"Indeed," Mona said, smiling. "Now I must get back to the kitchen. You know how to pick them, Tami," she said.

"Yes, isn't he handsome?" Tami said.

I could feel my face blushing.

It suddenly seemed odd to me that I was there at all. The reality of the situation hit me like the hunger knot growing in my stomach. I had just met this beautiful woman, half my age, and now another beautiful woman, nearer my age. They were as friendly as puppies. I had gone from being a lonely, depressed, senior citizen to a man seen in the eyes of two women as desirable. My emotions were more than slightly confused.

"Can I help you with something, Mom?" Tami asked as her mother left the room.

"I'm doing OK," Mona said. "Keep Kip company. Maybe he would like a drink?"

"Would you?" Tami asked.

"A beer would be fine," I said.

"He wants a beer, Mona,"

"Well get him one," Mona said.

Tami left the room and soon returned with two Coronas. She handed one to me and I twisted the top off and handed it back as she gave me the other. I twisted the top off of it and watched as Tami sipped the cold beer.

"Oh," she said, taking the beer away from her lips. "We should toast."

She held her beer out towards me.

"To good luck and good friends," she said.

"Skoal," I said. We clinked the bottles together and drank. The beer was cold and good. I felt the tension leaving me. I was no longer a lecher, a dirty old man seeking the companionship of a much younger woman. I was a friend.

Tami motioned again for me to sit.

She sat across from me, picked up a magazine and nonchalantly started to read.

I could faintly hear the sounds of a radio or television coming from the kitchen, and could smell what seemed like onions and peppers being sautéed in a skillet.

Suddenly the sizzling sound coming from the skillet, and the muffled sound of the TV were blanked by a piercing scream.

CHAPTER THREE

I jumped up and took three giant strides to the kitchen doorway. Then I heard it again. It was more like a screech than a scream. It sounded like Aieeee ek ek ek.

I nearly tripped on my flip-flops but managed to stay on my feet. Tami was suddenly at my side and we turned the corner into the kitchen neck and neck. I didn't know what to expect, maybe Mona had cut herself while dicing vegetables, saw a peeping tom through the window, or slipped and fell.

She stood there holding a piece of paper in her hand, staring at the screen of a small black and white TV. I glanced at the screen. There was a series of numbers displayed across the bottom and the words "Florida Power Vault Lotto" across the middle. I looked back at Mona. She was staring at the paper with a blank look on her face. The sound coming out of her mouth had changed from a screech to a giggle, then to a roaring laugh.

"Mom, what's wrong?" Tami asked.

"The lotto. I've won the lotto," Mona yelled, loud enough to be heard back on U.S. Highway One, a quarter of a mile away.

"You've what?"

"I've won the lotto, Tami. *I've won the LOTTO.*" Mona repeated. Then she repeated it again, her voice an octave higher and fifty decibels louder.

"Let me see," Tami said.

She took the scrap of paper and glanced from it to the TV and back to the paper, several times. I stood there transfixed at the scene being played out in the tiny kitchen.

"Hooray, you did!" Tami screamed suddenly.

"Let me see," I said, in shock.

Tami handed the paper to me and I read the series of numbers. Ten. Fourteen. Twenty-One. Seven. Thirty-Six. Then the words "Power Vault Number" then the number Nine.

I think I was watching the TV with one eye and reading the lotto ticket with the other, but suddenly something was wrong. The numbers disappeared from the TV screen and a man and woman were displayed. The man was saying, "That's the winning numbers for Florida's Power Vault lotto, worth one hundred and fourteen million dollars. More news when we return."

Then there was a Viagra commercial.

I wasn't sure that what I saw on the ticket was what was displayed on the TV. I turned to Tami. "They all matched?" I asked.

"All five and the power vault number," she said, grinning from ear to ear. Her white teeth gleamed in the sunlight now just peeking through the back kitchen window.

Mona started to weave back and forth and I took her arm to steady her.

"Are you all right?" I asked.

"I'm rich," was what she said. Then she screeched again, a pitch high enough and loud enough to cause me to back away.

A voice on the TV was admonishing viewers to ask their doctor if they were healthy enough for sex.

The immediate question in my mind was whether Mona was healthy enough to win the Florida Power Vault lotto. She was still swaying. Then it occurred to me that she wasn't about to fall, the sway was actually a hip wiggle, like a hula dancer.

She turned to me and grabbed me around the waist and with a force I wouldn't have believed possible from a woman her size, picked me up till I was on my tiptoes and whirled me around her small body.

"I'm rich," she screeched again. My eardrums felt as though I was at ground zero at Hiroshima.

"Take it easy, Mona," I said.

"Take it easy, Mom," Tami said.

She dropped me back to the flat of my feet and whirled away, dancing across the kitchen to Tami. She picked Tami completely off the floor and swung her around. One of Tami's hands swept a bottle of wine vinegar off of the kitchen counter and it hit the floor and shattered. Glass scooted everywhere and the immediate sweet-sour smell of the vinegar permeated the air.

That was enough to calm Mona down. She stopped whirling Tami, grabbed a broom from the corner and started to sweep broken glass. She looked down at the mess on the floor and smiled.

"I'll hire a maid to do things like this," she said. "No more scrubbing this floor for me!"

"No more tiny kitchen!" Tami said. "We'll build a house big enough to turn around in."

"Big enough to turn a semi-truck around in," Mona added. "God! Think about it. I'm rich." This time she didn't screech, she just stood there grinning.

"Are you sure you matched the numbers right?" I asked.

"I checked them, Kip," Tami said. "They're the winning numbers."

"What happens next?" I asked.

"It's too late to go to the lotto office today," Tami said. "They will be closed. Tomorrow we'll take the ticket in and have the money transferred to the bank."

"Then we'll buy a new car, new clothes, a round trip ticket to Tahiti, and when we come back we'll start building our new house," Mona said.

She looked at me. I still had the winning lotto ticket in my hand. One hundred and fourteen million dollars. The state and the federal government would get about half. That would still leave nearly $60 million.

"Can I have my ticket back, Kip?" she said, extending her hand.

I handed her the ticket. She turned a complete circle, glancing around the kitchen.

"Where can I put this where it will be safe?" she asked.

"Do you have a safe?" I asked.

"What would we be doing with a safe?" Tami asked me. "We've never had enough money to need a safe."

"Some people have them to protect valuable documents, computer discs, things like that." I said.

"I know," Mona said. "I'll put it in the breadbox. That's where we keep our household cash."

"Good idea, Mom," Tami said.

Mona walked to a small wooden box with a slanted lid. Putting the ticket on the counter, she raised the lid with one hand and took a loaf of bread out with the other. She exchanged the bread for the ticket, dropped it in the breadbox then put the loaf of bread on top of it and let the lid drop.

"It'll be safe there," she said, "Let's celebrate!"

"What will we do?" Tami asked.

"We'll go get a couple of bottles of good wine, finish fixing supper and sit and talk about what we can buy with the money," Mona said.

"We'll get the wine while you finish supper, Mom," Tami said.

She took me by the arm, guided me around the spilled vinegar and glass, and walked me to the living room.

"Can we take your car?" she asked, "And can I drive?"

I handed her the keys and opened the driver's side door. As I did I looked across the top of the car and saw a man walking through the palmettos toward the highway.

"Friend of yours?" I asked pointing towards the retreating figure.

Tami looked in the direction I was pointing but the figure had vanished.

"Where?" she queried.

I shaded my eyes and looked again. I was sure I had seen a man walking through the trees. Now I saw nothing but palm fronds swaying in the evening breeze.

"Never mind," I said. "Let's go get that wine."

****

CHAPTER FOUR

When I arrived at Dade County Central Hospital I was concerned about parking the Austin Healey in a municipal parking lot so I circled the area and found a pay lot, got the ticket from an automatic dispenser, waited for the bar to rise, and drove in. The pay lot was under a city building of some sort and I was glad to get out of the bright sun.

I walked the two blocks to the hospital entrance and asked for Tami's room at the reception area. As soon as I asked, the receptionist asked for my name. I gave her my card and she nodded to a uniformed police officer near the desk. He walked towards me and spoke my name.

"Kip Yardley?"

"That's me," I said. "What's the problem officer?"

I had been told that Tami was admitted to the hospital in a state of shock, and that she had my motel phone number programmed in her cell phone. I knew nothing else about the reason she was there.

"Can you come with me, Mr. Yardley?" the cop asked.

"Lead on Mac Duff," I said, congenially.

"I beg your pardon?" he said.

"Never mind," I responded. It was a standard utterance of mine when someone said something like "Can you come with me?" or "Follow me please."

I followed him to a room across a wide tiled floor. The word "Administration" was engraved on a black plaque on the door.

We went in. The outer office had a secretary's desk, a few file cabinets and four plain clothed cops. The inner office, to which I was led, had the hospital director and two more cops.

"Mr. Yardley?" one of the cops said, extending his hand. "I'm Detective Sergeant Happs."

"Why am I here, Detective Happs?" I asked, shaking his hand.

"You were at the home of Mona and Tami Fawn yesterday evening until late?"

"I was there until about one this morning," I said.

"Would you mind telling us the purpose of that visit?"

"I met Tami on the beach, she invited me home for supper."

"Do you know anything about what happened last night or sometime this morning?" he asked.

It was a loaded question. I knew about Mona Fawn winning the lotto. We had eaten supper, drank two bottles of wine and talked about cruises, home building, how to spend 60 million bucks. I said goodnight to the two ladies at 1 a.m. and drove back to my motel, took a shower and went to bed.

I told the detective that.

"Why am I here?" I asked again. "Has something happened that I should know about?"

"According to Tami Fawn," the detective said, grimacing as if it was hard to say the words, "her mother, Mona, won the lotto. This morning Tami found Mona in a grove of mangroves with her throat cut. She's dead."

I stood there staring at him in disbelief. The horror of his revelation was sinking into my head like the sun sinking in the Gulf of Mexico. I had worked cases where people were found dead. I had even put a man in that prone position with a shot through his left eye. Those memories were not pleasant and the gravity of those situations played havoc in my mind. Now I was being told that a beautiful woman that I had only known for a few hours was dead. She had been alive and wild with excitement the night before. I had helped her plan the vacation she had dreamed of her entire life. Now she's dead.

I looked around for a chair to sit on. My head was spinning and I could feel my pulse pounding through it.

"Would you like to sit down?" someone asked.

I nodded and someone pushed a straight-backed armless chair up to me. I sat down heavily.

"I knew Mona had the winning ticket to the lotto," I said. "I bought a couple of bottles of wine and we celebrated. I left about one a.m."

"Then you were one of the last people to see her alive," the detective said. "Did you see the lotto ticket?"

"Yeah, I had it in my hand. I checked the numbers against the ones on TV."

"What happened to the ticket, Mr. Yardley?"

"Why are you asking me?"

He reached in his shirt pocket and took out a pack of cigarettes, put one in his mouth and pulled out a lighter.

"No smoking in the hospital," he was reminded by someone.

"That kind of money is an awful temptation, Yardley," he said, dropping the mister and putting the cigarettes away.

"Wait a minute," I muttered. "You guys don't think I killed Mona for her lotto ticket?"

"We don't think anything," he said. "We're trying to piece together what might have happened."

"Well leave my piece out," I said. "You know who I am by now. You know I'm a PI from LA. Doesn't that give me any credence in your mind?"

"PI's have killed people for a lot less money, Yardley," he said.

"I saw Mona put the ticket in a breadbox in her kitchen," I told him. "That's the last I saw of it. It should still be there."

"Tami told us that too," he said. "It wasn't there."

I remembered the man I had seen walking through the mangrove trees when

Tami and I started to get in the Austin Healey. I told him about it.

"We'll check that out," he said. "In the meantime, hang around for a while, Yardley. I'll let you know if anything else comes up. Don't leave town till you hear from me."

I wasn't sure if I should remind him that he couldn't hold me without charge for more than 24 hours, but my better judgment made me remain silent. I hadn't planned on leaving right away and now I wanted to see Tami.

"I'd like to talk to Tami," I said.

"We'll have a nurse take you to her room," the hospital guy said.

"There'll be a policeman on duty outside her room," the detective told me. "If he stops you, tell him I cleared it."

I stood up and started to leave, looking around for the nurse that would lead me to Tami's room.

"One more thing, Yardley," I heard Detective Happs say.

When I turned to face him he handed me a folded paper. I knew without looking at it that it was a search warrant.

"That's a search warrant to search your room at the motel," he said.

"You'll find my gun in my suitcase," I said. "I've got permits."

"We won't take your gun, Yardley," he said. "Not yet anyway."

A pretty nurse entered the room and approached me.

"I'll take you to Tami Fawn's room now," she said.

I didn't respond with my standard "Lead on Mac Duff" this time.

CHAPTER FIVE

Tami was sitting in a chair next to a window, her back to me, when I entered her room, accompanied by the nurse and a uniformed cop.

"Mr. Yardley is here, Tami," the nurse said.

She turned and looked at me. The transformation that had occurred was shocking. Her dark eyes were lifeless and the whites were streaked with red. Her beautiful hair hung limp around her shoulders, the shade of coal dust. It was as if someone had inserted a needle into her heart and sucked out all of her life.

"Kip," she said, trying to smile at me. "I'm so glad you came."

"I've been told of your mother's death, Tami," I said, not really knowing what to say. "Of course I'll do anything I can to help you. Just name it."

"Find who killed Mona," she said, then her lips quivered and her eyes filled with tears. In seconds she was sobbing hysterically. She ran to me and threw her small arms around my waist and held on to me. I stood there a second looking down at the top of her head, and then put my arms around her. I couldn't find any words in the tangled cocoon that had formed in my mind.

My thoughts were racing. I had not intended to stay in the Miami area more than another three or four days. My plans were to head north, visit relatives in Kentucky and Illinois, and then back to California to my office, my staff and friends. Rhonda crossed my mind and I felt a twinge of pain in my chest. I was saddened by Tami's loss but now I felt guilty about the remorse at my own loss. Now wasn't the time to choke up on either. Tami needed my help. I knew, without a lot of thought that I would stay.

"I'll do my best, Tami," I said, holding her. I let her cry. There are times when we need to just let grief find its way into our hearts. If it can find a way in, it will eventually find its way out.

The pretty nurse told me that she and Tami were good friends, and that she would help Tami get dressed if she wanted to leave. The doctors had given her mild tranquilizers when the paramedics had brought her in. She had not slept and the questioning by

Detective Happs had taken a great toll on her.

"Can I go home now?" Tami asked me. I turned to the nurse. She nodded in the affirmative, and I gently released Tami and stepped back.

"I'll take you home if that's where you want to go," I said.

"Yes," she said. "I can't put it off. I've got to face it."

"I'll wait outside until you're ready," I said, and turned away.

"Kip?" she said.

I turned and looked at her.

"Thank you," she said and tried to smile at me.

I winked at her and then felt silly about it but I didn't know what else to do. Once before in my life I had held a young woman in my arms as she screamed and wept. It was different, though. A killer had abducted that young woman and she had just watched me put a slug through the killer's brain.

I left the room and waited outside with the uniformed officer.

Fifteen minutes later Tami and the nurse came out. Tami looked very nice. She had showered and washed her hair. It hung wet and wavy around her shoulders. Her face had gained some color and her eyes appeared a little more lifelike and clear.

"Take good care of her," the nurse told me.

"I will," I said.

"Thanks, Gerri," Tami said to the nurse. "I'll call you."

"OK," the nurse said. "Remember, I am off tomorrow so if you need me to come over, I'll be glad to."

The two girls hugged and we left the ward, took the elevator back to the lobby and headed for the door. I remembered that I had parked two blocks away and offered to go get the car and come back for her, but Tami insisted on walking with me.

"I thought I'd never get out of there," she told me. "They questioned me like they thought I killed Mona."

"I'm very sorry about Mona," I said, again not knowing just what words to use.

"For a while I was more angry than sad," she told me. "Was I wrong to feel that way, Kip?"

I knew exactly what she was telling me, but had no words to form a reply.

"It's OK," was all that came out of my mouth.

"No, it is not OK," she told me. "I found my Mom dead. Her throat had been cut. It's not going to be OK until the person who killed her pays for it."

"I'm sorry, Tami. I didn't mean that it was OK that Mona was killed. I meant it's OK the way you felt anger. I can feel that anger too and I hardly knew her."

"Oh, Kip," she took my hand and stopped. I turned and looked at her. "Please forgive me. I shouldn't yell at you."

I gave her a faint smile. "I know, Tami."

"You will help me find her killer?" she asked.

"Yes." I said.

"And if we find the lotto ticket, I'll share it with you."

"Detective Happs told me it wasn't in the breadbox."

"She may have moved it," Tami said.

"We'll look for it," I told her.

"Oh the hell with the lotto ticket," Tami said suddenly. "Where do we start to look for the killer?"

I mentioned the man I thought I had seen the night before.

"It may not be anything," I said. "I'd like to see if I could find that guy, though. I would like to know if he saw anything. Any idea who it might have been?"

"No, Kip," she said. "We are pretty isolated back there. I've seen people in the mangroves before; sometimes they walk through there like they are looking for something. It may have been just some guy looking for mushrooms or snakes."

"Snakes?" I said.

"Yes. There are people who capture snakes and milk them for their venom. They sell the venom to the medical profession."

I thought about that. "That isn't something I would do," I said.

We had covered the two blocks as we talked and I opened the passenger door of the Healey.

"Thank you, sir," she said.

I thought I could hear a little more life in her voice.

"I'm curious to know how anyone else but the three of us, you, Mona, and I, knew that she had a winning lotto ticket," I said.

"Do you think someone killed her for the lotto ticket?" she asked.

"That seems to be what the police think." I said. "They told me it was a powerful motive."

"But how would anyone know she won?"

"That's what I want to know." I said. "That's probably the second area of investigation we should look at, after I find the guy that I saw on your place last evening."

The Austin Healey engine started with the musical, vibrating roar that I loved to hear. We left the underground parking lot and I headed the car towards Tami's home.

CHAPTER SIX

I could tell that Tami wanted to be alone, as soon as we reached her place. It wasn't anything she said, it was the way she looked. I helped her out of the car and walked into the house with her. I could still faintly smell the aroma of peppers, onions and meat that had been fixed for dinner the previous night.

"I'll be back in a couple of hours," I said. "I'll bring something to eat when I come back."

She smiled at me with a sad smile. "O.K." was all she said.

I got back in the Healey and left. I drove slowly back down the lane that led to Tami and Mona's place, looking to my left into the mangroves, palmettos and saw grass to see if I could estimate the spot where I saw the figure of a man the night before. About half way to the main road I noticed a trail that led back to my left into the grass. I pulled the Healey to my right, slightly off the road, and killed the engine. I sat for a few minutes, listening, and watching the grove to my left.

Satisfied that nothing was afoot or about, unless it was crawling, I left the Healey and followed the narrow trail. I didn't like the idea of walking through that area without high top leather shoes, and my Nike sneakers didn't provide much protection from snakes, but I watched ahead of me and took careful steps. Nothing was moving.

The trail intersected another trail that ran parallel to the road, at a point 50 yards or so into the grove of trees. I looked right, towards town, then left towards Tami's place, and mentally flipped a coin. Heads I go right, tails, I go left. I chose heads and turned right. A half a dozen steps further I found a cigarette butt. It was just the filter. I froze in the trail and knelt on both knees looking around the area. My eyes aren't what they used to be, but a foot or so from the cigarette filter I saw a tiny ball of paper. Someone had carefully field stripped the cigarette, breaking the remaining tobacco and paper from the filter, scattering the tobacco, and rolling the paper into a tiny ball. I carefully unrolled the ball and spread it out between my fingers. It had been a Marlboro light.

Could have belonged to anyone, I thought, but it might have been smoked by the man I had seen walking that trail the evening before Tami found Mona dead.

I dropped the paper and walked carefully ahead, not really knowing what I was looking for and not expecting to find anything.

It took me the better part of a half hour to follow the trail out to where it intersected a road. I knew that road would intersect the one that I had parked the Healey on, so I turned right and walked down the edge. Two cars passed me, each slowing, the occupants gawking at me, wondering why anyone would be walking in the heat of a Florida afternoon. I passed a service station on my left that I recognized and knew that I was close to Tami's road.

As I walked I was thinking about the lotto ticket. Someone had to know that Mona put the ticket in the breadbox. The kitchen was not disturbed. No drawers had been pulled out; the cupboards had not been ransacked. There were no cupboard doors left open. One of two scenarios played in my mind. Either someone had been watching through the kitchen window or Mona told someone where the ticket was hidden.

My instincts told me it was the first. But how had the thief got in? I was reasonably sure that two women living alone out in the boonies would not have gone to bed and left their house unlocked. There were no signs of forced entry. That meant that Mona or Tami had let someone in or Mona had taken the ticket out of the breadbox and left the house with it.

I guess I must have been so engrossed in my thoughts that I had wondered out onto the road a little and a passing motorist interrupted my thoughts by beeping his horn at me. I jumped, a little startled, and then realized I had reached Tami's road so I turned right and concentrated on my walk. It was hot and I would rather be driving the Healey than walking the side road. Twenty minutes later I was in the car, air conditioner going full blast, and headed for the market where Tami and I had purchased the wine.

CHAPTER SEVEN

There were two other customers in the store ahead of me. I didn't really need gas but pulled to the tanks and topped off the Austin Healey. It took about five gallons to top it off and I replaced the nozzle in the hook and sauntered in.

One of the customers, a gray haired lady who had driven in to the parking lot in a golf cart, was chatting with the clerk.

"You just don't know who you can trust anymore," she was saying. "That woman was going to be rich, and now she's dead."

"Yes, it's a shame, Mrs. Winistaus," the clerk said.

"The TV says that the lotto ticket she bought is missing."

"That's what I heard," the clerk said.

"How would they know it was hers if someone turned it in?" Mrs. Winistaus asked. I perked up my ears. I was curious to know the answer to that question.

"It would be on the ticket where it was bought," the clerk said. "And besides it was the only one with all the right numbers."

The second customer, a rough looking guy with a tank top shirt, tattoos and a scar across his forehead, shuffled his feet and held up a six-pack of beer.

"Well I hope they catch whoever killed her," Mrs. Winistaus was saying, ignoring the motion made by the tough guy.

I sidled away from the counter, picked up a small bag of Fritos, walked to the cooler and got a Pepsi in a can. I could still hear the buzzing of Mrs. Winistaus voice from the back of the store. Eventually she left and tough guy paid for his beer and left.

"Will there be anything else?" the clerk asked me.

"No thanks," I said. "Do they know where that winning ticket was sold?"

"I know," she said, and smiled at me. "I'm pretty sure it was sold right here."

"How would you know that?" I asked.

"I ran a check to see if there were any winners yesterday. I do that every morning after the lotto closes. The computer showed one winner. It didn't pinpoint this store but it shows that it was sold by a 7-11 here in Homestead. There used to be two more 7-11's here, but one burned last year and was never rebuilt. The other one has been closed for a while. Their gas tanks were leaking and they closed. I'm not sure if they are open now or not. Or they might have just quit selling gas, I don't know. That leaves this store."

"Did you know the woman who was killed?" I asked.

"Mona?" she said. "Yes, I knew her when I saw her. We were never close friends, but she stopped here a lot to buy lotto tickets and grocery items. Her husband died last year. I think she has a daughter who is a nurse."

"But you don't remember selling her a ticket yesterday?"

"No, but then I wasn't here yesterday. Sharon was on duty yesterday. I had to take my kid to a doctor. He's going to play basketball at school and they have to have a check up and be released by a doctor before they can play."

"What time do lotto ticket sales end?" I asked.

"We can't sell tickets after 8 on the day of the drawing," she told me.

I paid for my gas and the Fritos and Pepsi and left the store.

A man was standing near my Austin Healey. I walked to the car and opened the door.

"Nice car," he said. "I used to have one of these. It was right after I got back from the service."

I had heard that before. Sometimes the speaker has indeed owned an Austin Healey. Other times they've wished they had owned one. I've even had guys tell me they owned one and found out they had been wannabee MG owners. Anyone who has ever owned a Healey will never mistake it for an MG and vice versa.

"I like it," I said and opened the door.

"I'm going to buy me another one someday," the man said. I looked a little closer at him. He was dressed in shorts with a flowery short sleeved shirt, buttoned twice, exposing a paunch of a belly. He was of medium build, deeply tanned and clean-shaven.

"Don't suppose you could give me a ride?" he asked.

"I'm kind of busy," I said.

"Oh I don't live far," he told me. "I wouldn't ask, but it's hard for me to walk sometimes." He took a few steps and I could see that he was limping. I didn't know how much of the limp was real and how much was faked, but I was polite enough to ask.

"Bad leg?"

"You could say that," he grinned. "There's no leg there."

He reached down and pointed to his lower right leg. I looked closer and could see that it was a slightly different shade of tan than the left one. It had a shiny look to it. Plastic.

"Get in," I said.

He smiled broadly and walked around the car without nearly as much limp as he had in the few steps that he had made previously. He opened the door and climbed in, pulled his right leg in after him and closed the door.

"I appreciate this," he said, grinning. "My name is ValJean DuPont. People call me Val."

"Hello, Val," I said, extending a hand. He shook it with a firm grip.

"I'm walking today," he said. "My truck is in the shop for service. I can't stand to be cooped up all day, had to get out and walk."

"Where to?" I asked.

"Oh, just make a left out of the parking lot and I'll tell you when to turn. I live down at the bay."

I followed his instructions and the Austin Healey purred out onto the road, crossed the road that Tami lived on, and I shifted gears and let the six cylinder engine drink heavily from the three carburetors. It gave off the distinct mellow roar that makes Healey lovers grin like eating watermelons and spitting seeds.

"What year was your Healey?" I asked.

"A fifty five," he said. "It was a 100-4. What year is this one?"

"Sixty two," I said. "One of about two thousand made. It's got three carbs, center shift tranny. That makes it pretty rare."

"Nice," he said, grinning.

We rode in silence for a few minutes, I was waiting for directions, but none came.

"Didn't I see your car out at Mona's?" he asked. That caught me off guard.

"When was that?" I asked.

"Earlier today," he said. "Half an hour or more before I saw it at the 7-11."

"That was me," I said. "Would you have passed it on the road walking?"

"Yeah," he said, and remained silent.

A few minutes later he told me to make a right at a fork in the road and less than a quarter of a mile further we came to the bay.

"This is where I live," he said. "There's my home right there."

He pointed to a strange looking vessel drifting on tether to a dock. It looked like a large raft with half of a geodesic dome built of plywood. Solar panels were attached to the plywood parts of the dome. Lines hung across one end of the raft with what appeared to be vinyl bags attached.

He opened the door and got out.

"Come on in," he told me, "I'll buy you a drink."

"I'm in a bit of a hurry," I said.

"Nonsense!" he told me. "I'd like to buy you a drink. I have one about this time every day. Just a quick drink. Won't hurt you none."

I hesitated, but then thought that I really didn't know what my next move would be anyway, finally said what the heck, and got out of the car. We went aboard the raft and entered the dome shaped structure. It was cool inside, although the temperature outside was nearing 90. I could hear a faint hum. He snapped on a light, opened a small refrigerator and got out ice. From a cabinet below a kitchen sink he extracted a bottle of dark looking liquor and two glasses. He put three cubes of ice in each glass and poured them half full of the booze.

"I make it myself," he said proudly. "Bottoms up!"

I took a sip. It was strong but pleasant. I knew it was some kind of dark rum made from sorghum cane. Potent, but potable.

"How do you know Mona and Tami?" I asked.

"I knew Mona before I went in the service," he told me. "We went out a few times back in those days. Then I went overseas and she got married. I guess she forgot about me after I left." He looked sideways at me for a second, then away. "Never good at women anyway." He said with an air of finality.

"Any idea who might have wanted to kill her?" I asked.

"No-one." He said. "She was a kind person. Everybody liked her."

"Did you lose your leg in the war?" I asked.

"I'd rather not talk about that," he said abruptly. "I've been alone since I got back. I don't tell anyone what happened. There's stories going around, but I aint told anyone."

I noticed a distinct clip to his voice as if he suddenly wished he hadn't invited me to share his noonday drink. I sipped hard at my drink till it was gone and then swirled the ice in the empty glass.

"Thanks for the drink," I said. "I'm glad to meet you, Val."

"You aint told me your name," he reminded me.

"It's Kip Yardley," I said. "My full name is Rudyard Kipling Yardley, but people just call me Kip."

"Thanks for the ride, Kip," he said. "I hope I see you again someday."

I left the room, passed over the deck and across the dock. I glanced back once and saw him watching me. I made a mental note to ask Tami about him. I was surprised that I had told him my full name. I don't remember ever telling anyone my full name before.

CHAPTER EIGHT

I drove back to my motel room and checked to see what, if anything, had been disturbed by the police when they searched my room. Everything appeared in order. My gun was in its case, inside my suitcase. Clothes that I had removed and hung in the proper spot were still hanging. I noticed that they hadn't disturbed my shoes; other than flip-flops, I only had four pair with me, two pairs of sneakers, a pair of hiking boots and a pair of dress shoes. My only suit hung on its hanger, pants folded and held to the bar by the little extra wooden piece that is provided on most motel hangers.

I hadn't had time for a shower when the hospital called so I put on a bathing suit, took a quick dip in the motel swimming pool, then showered and put on clean clothes. Then I headed the Healey towards the police station. There were some questions I was going to ask that I hoped someone might be able to answer.

I found Detective Happs without difficulty. His office was neat and tidy, and he sat behind a standard metal desk, nothing fancy, but adequate. I knocked on his open door.

He looked up and motioned me to come in.

"Mr. Yardley," he said. He didn't get up or offer his hand, but instead waved me to a seat on the opposite side of his desk.

"Hello, Detective," I said. "Do you have time to talk to me about Mona Fawn?"

"I've got nothing but time," he sighed. "No leads, no lotto ticket, and the press is on my ass for a story."

"Then you won't mind if I ask a few questions?"

"Ask away, my man," he said. "I don't mind telling you what I know if you promise to keep me posted on anything you might dig up."

"Deal," I said.

"Ask away," he said again.

"First, can you tell me anything about Mona Fawn, other than the lotto ticket, that might have got her in trouble?"

"Meaning?" he asked.

"Drugs? Any record? History of arrests or disturbances?"

"Nope."

"What about her late husband?"

"Josh Hayden? He was a quiet man. Never had a bit of trouble at home or as far as I can tell, anywhere else. Never arrested. Not a drug user. Drank a little, but not an alcoholic. Clean as a whistle."

I was silent for a few seconds so he spoke.

"You think I haven't gone over all of this stuff already?" he asked.

"I figured you had," I said. "This is just for my own knowledge."

"Well, you're pretty good," he said. "Were you a cop?"

"Highway Patrol," I said. "Assigned for a while with homicide."

"Figures," he said. "Anything else you want to ask?"

"Have you got anything from the coroner? What time did she die, what was the official cause of death? Any unusual marks on the body?"

"She died at 4 a.m. or thereabouts, according to the coroner. Her throat was cut, severing the Carotid Artery she bled to death within seconds. Officially she died of massive bleeding. Nothing unusual about the body. No identifying marks, no tattoos, needle marks, bruises or other wounds."

"Was she killed where she was found?"
I asked.

"Not far away," he said. "Coroner's boys found a spot near the water where she was attacked. She was dragged to the spot where her daughter found her. The body was fully clothed except for shoes. No shoes were found in the vicinity. The crime scene boys didn't find anything that aroused their attention. I don't have the pictures but when I get them I'll be glad to show them to you."

"How about tracks?" I asked.

"Tide washed out the tracks at the spot where she was killed," he said. "Some tracks where she was dragged back into the mangrove thicket. Approximately size 10 shoes, sneakers. I had my guys make plaster casts. I'll have them here tomorrow if you'd like to see them."

"How about friends, associates, former employers?"

"Mona never held a job," he said. "She inherited the land where her house is, and her parents left her a small amount of money. They died while she was still in high school. Mona got pregnant her sophomore year and dropped out of school, had the baby and stayed home to take care of it. The father skipped out and she never told anyone who he was. Rumor has it that he joined the army."

"You say she was a sophomore when she dropped out?" I asked.

"Yep."

"That's funny," I said, remembering something Tami had told me. "She couldn't read or write?"

"I don't know anything about that," he said. "How did she get to be a sophomore if she couldn't read or write?"

"Good question," I said. "That's exactly what I wanted to know."

He didn't answer or offer any solution, so I asked the next question on my list.

"How about siblings?"

"Mona was an only child," he said. "Not even cousins, aunts or uncles, as far as I can tell."

I had pretty much reached a cul-de-sac in my list of questions.

"Is there a library around here that I might use for some research?" I asked.

"Right down the highway from Mona's place," he said. "Take the road leading away from the bay, past the 7-11 where Mona bought the ticket and about two miles out you'll see the library on the right."

"She did buy the ticket there?" I asked, surprised that he would know.

"According to the clerk on duty," he said. "We interviewed her at her home early this morning."

"The same clerk that's on duty today?" I asked.

"No, a girl named Sharon. She sold Mona the ticket."

"One more question," I said. "I met a man named ValJean DuPont. He knows Tami and Mona. Do you have anything on him?"

"He's harmless," Detective Happs said. "A veteran. There's a wild story going around. People say he was a medic in the war but got home without a scratch. Then he was in the swamps fishing when a gator chomped down on his leg."

"He pulled a pistol and shot the gator but it wouldn't let go of his leg. The story is that he cut off his own leg. Takes a brave man to cut off one of his legs. But desperate men do desperate things, I guess."

I thanked him and left his office.

CHAPTER NINE

I found the library without difficulty and sat for an hour going through old Homestead High yearbooks. I found Tami in one of the yearbooks, but it was Mona I was really looking for. I thought that Tami would have been about 18 when she graduated from high school, so I went back 18 years and started looking at yearbooks at that point. Mona wasn't in any of the graduating classes but I found her as a sophomore. She was cute, tiny for her age, and, from all indications, popular. She was vice president of her class, belonged to the cheer leading squad, and active in Thespians. Strange for someone who couldn't read or write.

The yearbook for the following year did not have Mona in it. So she had dropped out of school that year, like the cop told me, and had a baby.

I went back to the year before and looked at the class picture again where Mona was vice president. There were twenty-two students in her homeroom, 14 boys and 8 girls. I looked at the boys, trying to find one that I thought might be Tami's father. There was no real resemblance to any. I jotted down the names on a piece of scrap paper, and then went to the next year. All of them appeared in the next yearbook.

Detective Happs had said that the father of Tami had skipped out and joined the Army. None of Mona's classmates had skipped out; they were all in the next year's yearbook. That meant that the father either hadn't attended school in Homestead, or was a few years older.

I went back to the yearbook with Mona as a sophomore and wrote down the names of the boys who were juniors that year. There were 19 boys who were juniors. The following year, all but one was in the senior class. The one who was missing was ValJean DuPont. Had I found Tami's birth father?

I soon got tired of guessing about Tami's father and asked the librarian for the genealogy section. She pointed me in the direction of a glassed in room, gave me a key and asked me to leave any books that I might remove from shelves on the table, the staff would replace them.

I found an old telephone book of early Homestead residences and looked up the name Fawn. There were two Fawns, one named Carlos and the other was Harold. In an index of local cemeteries, I found Harold Fawn, born in 1940 died in 1979; in the same plot was Hannah D. Fawn, born 1941 died 1979. These two must have been the parents of Mona.

I located an index of obituaries for 1979 in the Homestead Journal and soon was reading news clipping about the unfortunate demise of Harold and Hannah Fawn. Harold had been a computer programmer and had started his own firm shortly after leaving college. By the mid seventies he had amassed a respectable estate, purchased two hundred acres of land and built a comfortable home on it.

In 1979 Harold and Hannah had taken a trip to New York in his private airplane. On their return to Homestead the aircraft crashed and burned on a dense mountaintop in the Blue Ridge range of northern Georgia, shortly after refueling in South Carolina. The cause of the crash was never determined.

The article went on to say that Mona Fawn, daughter of Harold and Hannah Fawn, would be in the custody of her grandfather, Carlos Fawn, a retired railroad employee, living in nearby Dade county.

Carlos Fawn's wife, Maria, had died the year before.

On a hunch, I looked on a library computer for the Lotto Commission for the State of Florida. I had an idea in the back of my mind. If they (the Lotto Commission) could tell who bought a ticket, why was the printed ticket needed to collect the money? Maybe there was a way I could help Tami collect the lotto winnings.

I found the website without any difficulty and learned that the Lotto Commissioner's name was Oliver La Feur. A governor whose term had expired several years before had appointed him; the appointment was for life. That meant that if La Feur was still alive, he was still the commissioner.

There was a "contact us" link on the home page so I clicked on it and was taken to a page that had a list of phone numbers. The offices were in Leon County, at the capitol of Florida, Tallahassee. I used my cell phone and called the number. It took me five minutes to get through to the head cheese, Mr. La Feur himself, and he answered with a gruff hello.

"Lotto, Ollie La Feur speaking," he said with a deep base voice that sounded like it was coming from the bottom of a 55 gallon drum.

I introduced myself and asked the question that was the reason for my call.

"I hate to be the one to tell you this, Mr. Yardley," he said, although I could hear no remorse in his voice. "The rules specifically state that the lotto ticket must be presented at this office within 180 days in order for payment to be made."

"What happens at the end of the 180 days if no one turns in the ticket?" I asked.

"Well part of the money rolls over to the next drawing," he said.

I thanked him and hung up.

I forgot to ask him what happens to the other part of the money.

CHAPTER TEN

By late afternoon I had exhausted all of the ideas that had crept into my head. I was feeling tired. The fish sandwich I had for lunch was long since gone and my appetite had started to clamor. I thought about my promise to Tami to bring back something to eat.

I drove back to Tami's residence without stopping to get anything to eat. I'll just take her out to dinner somewhere, I thought. No foods I had thought of to take back sounded good to me. When I am really hungry the first thing I think of is Mexican Food. Southern California is full of very good Mexican restaurants. I didn't know about Florida.

I knocked and Tami let me in, taking my hand and ushering me into the kitchen. She stopped and put her hands on my chest and looked up at me with those beautiful eyes.

"I'm glad you didn't bring anything back," she said. "Can we go out to eat somewhere? I need to get out of this house for a while."

"Sure, Tami," I said. "Where would you like to go?"

"You name it," she said.

"Do you know of a good Mexican place?"

"Yes," she said. "I'll drive, if you don't mind."

I gave her the keys to the Healey and we left, locking the house.

She drove the car with a little more command than she had the previous day when we went out for wine. She let it out in each gear, shifted effortlessly, and maintained a speed five miles or so past the speedlimit. I had the top down and the wind blew her hair back away from her face. The Miami moon was shining and she looked lovely in the early evening light.

I wasn't watching the road as much as I was watching Tami. She must have seen the big vehicle approach from our left, I didn't see it. She hit the brakes sharply, at the same time she cut the wheel hard right. The big car flew by in front of us and Tami cut the wheel back left and went on through the intersection. The light was still green in our favor.

"Idiot!" she yelled at the car speeding away.

"He ran a red light," was all I could say.

"I know," she said. "I saw him coming. He was driving way too fast to stop. Good thing I saw him."

I was thankful that she had been watching because my attention had been completely on how nice she looked. I didn't see the car approaching at all.

"You handled the car like a pro," I told her.

"A former boyfriend was a NASCAR driver," she said. "He taught me a few things about driving."

"Thank God for that," I told her.

A short way up the highway she turned into a parking lot. I could see a large red neon sign that read "Hot To Molly" and underneath it a smaller blue neon sign that read, "Mexican Food".

She parked the car and I put a dead stick on the steering wheel and around the brake pedal, pulled it tight and locked it. A car like the Healey would be a prize for any car thief. I knew that the dead stick wouldn't stop a thief that had a lot of time, but it would certainly slow down one for an hour or so.

We were seated immediately and I ordered a margarita for Tami and a Dos Equis beer. The drinks arrived and both of us had decided what we wanted to eat. The waiter took our order and while we waited for our food I started to make a conversation.

"Tami, do you know anything about your grandparents, Harold and Hannah?"

"Only that they were killed in a plane crash when Mona was in high school," she said. "That's about all."

"How about Carlos?"

"I found a book once that had been written by a local journalist. In it he portrayed Carlos as someone having connections with New York mob."

"Was it fiction or written as a factual book?" I asked, my interest piqued.

"He wrote the book about Mafia influence in the real estate market in Florida," she said. "The passage I remember was very short. It said that there were a few people who were influential with union construction workers. One of the ones named was Carlos Fawn."

"Do you still have the book?" I asked.

"Unless Mona got rid of it," she said. "I found it in a box of junk in the garage. It may still be there."

"Do you remember the author?"

"I'm not sure, but I think his name was Letchman. I can't remember his first name."

I started to ask another question but she interrupted me.

"A" she said. "B..C..D"

I sat wondering what she was doing.

When she got to E she stopped. "Emory," she said.

"Emory?"

"Yes. The author's name was Emory Letchman."

She laughed, a little tinkling sound.

"You should have seen the look on your face," she said.

"When you started reciting the alphabet?"

"I do that when I can't think of someone's name," she told me. "I start with A, then think if that is what the name started with, then I go on to B and so forth, eventually I'll think of it."

"Emory Letchman," I said. "If you can't find the book at home, I can get it from the library."

Our food came and the waiter placed it in front of us.

Enchiladas and beans and rice is my favorite dish. I ate with gusto and watched as Tami picked at her tamales.

"Is your food OK?"

"It's fine," she said. "I was just thinking. Mom used to love to come here. Josh used to bring us here before he died."

I remained silent. There are times when no matter what a person says, it isn't enough, or it's too much. I let her have her thoughts. After a few minutes her solemn attitude appeared to leave. She finished eating and drank the last of her margarita.

"I'm finished,' she told me. "If you want to leave now, we can go."

As we left the restaurant I asked her if she wanted to drive home, and she declined.

I opened her door for her and after she got in I shut it and started back around to the drivers side door when I saw two young men walking towards me. They looked intent on reaching me before I got in the car, so I opened the door then stood next to it, waiting to see what transpired.

"Nice car," one of them said.

I waited.

As they walked closer, I turned to face them and took a stance that would let me move in any direction except back. My back was to the car door. The one who spoke walked straight towards me, the other one angled off as if he were going to the passenger side.

"Whatever you've got on your mind, don't do it," I told them, my voice a little louder than normal.

"Whadya mean, old man?" the first guy to speak asked.

He was close enough now that I could see his face plainly. He was probably not older than twenty, just a few scraggly looking hairs on his chin that I guessed he thought made him look masculine. I watched the other guy out of the corner of my eye.

"That's close enough," I said, a little louder.

"We just want to see your car, Grampus," the speaker said.

"You can see it from there," I told him.

"I'd like to sit in the drivers seat," he said. I could smell his breath, he was so close.

"Back off, kid," I told him.

"What's up, Grampus, you 'fraid we'll take your cunt?"

That did it.

He didn't even see my left foot snap at his crotch. By the time he realized I'd kicked him in the balls I had hit him twice with my fist, once in the middle of his eyes and once right where his ribs met in the middle.

He fell backwards stumbling but regained his balance as the other one started back towards me.

"Now you've got a problem, old man," the other guy said.

I waited until he took a swing at me, a wild roundhouse swing that might have did some serious damage had I not seen it coming from two miles away. It was an easy block. I blocked with a left inside block, knocking his hand and arm across his body, half spinning as I got my left foot planted. Then I kicked him on the left side of his head with my right foot.

Number one charged me like a bull. I moved slightly to my right, turned my right side towards him and grabbed his left arm, jerking it in the direction he traveled. He lunged past me and I brought my left knee up hard into his crotch. That took the fight out of him.

He bounced off of the drivers side back fender of the Healey and fell to his knees holding his private parts. The second goon was getting up. I sent a sidekick into his right kneecap and heard a satisfying snap as his knee buckled the wrong way. He went down with a thud.

I got in the car, shut the door, unlocked the dead stick and started the engine.

"Next time we meet, watch your mouth," I said.

As I dove away, Tami turned and shouted:

"And don't call him 'Old Man"!"

We were blocks away when it started to sink in. The two young punks weren't just out looking for a fight, they knew who I was and were trying to send me a message of some sort. If they were just looking for a fight, they would have been sitting in my car when we got to the parking lot.

It was just a passing thought, but enough of a nag on my thought processes to keep me quiet. Tami noticed the silence and asked me if I was OK.

"Oh, I'm fine. A little winded. I'm not as young as I once was."

"You're not an old man, though," she said. "I loved the way you handled those two punks."

"Do you mind if we go by my motel for a minute?" I asked.

"Why Kip," she said. "Are you going to seduce me?"

The thought hadn't entered my mind. There was another reason I wanted to go by my room. My 9MM Star was there. The two punks who had been aggressive were easy. The next ones might not be so easy.

"I'm going to take a rain check on that," I said.

"Maybe you *are* an old man," she said, laughing.

I didn't want to tell her that I was going to pick up my gun. I didn't want to frighten her by saying what I suspected about the two punks being sent to relay a message. It was just a feeling, not a fact that I was sure of. I laughed too, although my heart was really not in it.

I drove to the motel and got out. I didn't ask Tami in, nor did I walk around and open her door for her.

"Be right back," I said.

I was a little worried that the two might have been sent to delay me long enough for someone to go through my room. Whoever killed Mona would probably know about me and they might have wanted to search my room for the lotto ticket. I was concerned that if they did, they would find my gun.

The door was locked. When I unlocked it with my card I pushed it open, waited a full five seconds, stuck my arm around the edge of the door and turned the light on without entering. I could see into the room and nothing had been disturbed. I took three fast, long steps into the room and glanced quickly left and right. No one was there to surprise me.

I dug my 9MM out of my suitcase and stuck it in my waistband, pulling my shirt down over it. It would show if someone was looking right at it, but I didn't think Tami would notice.

Back in the car, I started the engine. Tami was looking at me with a quizzical look on her face.

So I was wrong. The two punks had not been sent to slow me down. Maybe they were just two kids looking for a fight.

CHAPTER ELEVEN

The instant that Tami opened the door to her house I knew something was wrong. There was a light on in the kitchen and I remembered turning it off as we walked towards the front door to go eat.

Tami stopped and looked around the living room. She gave out a slight little yell and I flipped on the light. The room was a mess. Someone had ripped open the seat cushions of the couch and chair, pulled drawers out and dumped them on the floor. The base was removed from a floor lamp. End tables were turned upside down.

"Call 9-1-1" I told her and walked on into the kitchen.

It was a bigger mess. Sugar and flour were on the cabinet tops and floor. Canned goods were scattered in front of cupboards. The refrigerator door stood open. The ice trays had been removed and melting ice was on the counter tops. Cereal had been poured out of the containers onto counter tops. Nothing remained untouched, it seemed.

I heard Tami talking and walked back to the living room.

"You're going to send someone out?" she was asking.

I couldn't hear the party on the other end of the line but Tami was shaking her head up and down. She muttered "thank you" and hung up.

"Kip, they've killed Mona and now they have ruined my house!"

She started to cry. I put my arms around her and held her close to me. She sobbed silently and I stroked her back with my hands. She put her arms around me and when she felt my gun, she jerked away from me.

"You are carrying your gun?" she asked.

"That's why I went to my motel room," I said. "I don't think those boys were out looking for a fight. Now I think they were trying to detain us while somebody did this." I swept my arm around the room.

"They were looking for the lotto ticket," Tami said.

"More than likely," I admitted. "Is there anywhere else that Mona might have hid it that hasn't been searched?"

"I doubt it," she said. "I'll look in her room."

She went to one of the doors leading off of the hallway and opened it. I saw the light go on, then heard her start crying again.

I went to her and saw that the bedroom had been searched thoroughly.

"Whoever did this didn't find anything," I said.

"How can you know that?" she asked.

"They would have stopped looking once they found it," I said. "I'll bet your room has been searched too."

We looked. I was right.

"Will they be back?" she asked.

"No," I said, convinced. "They didn't find it and they don't think they will find it here. Whoever did this did a good job. I couldn't have searched this place any more thoroughly than it has been searched."

We went back to the kitchen and Tami started the long process of cleaning up the mess.

"I've got to go to the funeral home tomorrow and make arrangements," she said. "Now I've got this mess to clean up.'

"I'll help you," I said. I started picking things up, putting canned goods back on shelves, straightening things.

"I can do it, Kip," she said. "You don't have to stay."

"I'm not leaving you tonight," I told her. "I'll sleep on the couch. You might not be safe alone."

"I'll be OK," she said. "It'll take me half the night to clean this place up, you don't have to stay."

"No argument," I told her. "I'm staying.'

"OK" she told me. "But you don't have to sleep on the couch. You can sleep in my bed."

I was momentarily shocked by that until she explained.

"I'll sleep in Mona's room."

CHAPTER TWELVE

The police arrived and it surprised me that Detective Happs was with them.

We exchanged hellos and Happs sat talking to Tami while I continued to clean the kitchen. I wasn't really listening to the questions Happs was asking and it surprised me when he came to the kitchen door and asked me about the hassle at the restaurant.

"Tami told you about that?" I asked.

"Yep," he said. "She said you think you might have been held up, time wise, to give whoever did this a chance to get it done?"

"That thought crossed my mind," I said.

"Someone called 9-1-1 about the fight," he told me. "When we got there the two punks were gone. Can you describe them?"

I gave him a rundown on what the two boys looked like. My training has given me a sense of observation that is greater than most. I remembered almost every detail of the incident, right down to the fact that the skinny kid that approached me had breath that smelled like two day old salami. I remembered seeing a tattoo on his neck. It was a chain of stars that went all the way around his neck. He was about six foot tall, a hundred and fifty pounds. He wore a white tee shirt, levis, pointed toe shoes and his hair was combed down on the sides and spiked in the middle like a Mohawk.

Happs took the description on a small tape recorder rather than writing it down. The details of the house burglary attempt was all down on paper, written by a uniformed officer.

I described the second attacker with almost as much detail, but hadn't got close to him except when he swung at me. I remembered seeing an earring in his right ear. No tattoos. Five foot ten, one eighty. Light brown or blond hair, combed straight back and tied in a pony tail.

"If you think of anything else, call me," he said, giving me his card.

He handed one to Tami. "You too," he said. "If you discover something missing, or remember something, give me a call. If you have any more incidents like the one at the Mexican place, call me first. If you can't forestall anything long enough to call me, then kick the bastards a couple of times for me."

He smiled, shook my hand and Tami's and he and the uniformed officer left.

CHAPTER THIRTEEN

I slept restlessly, waking up at the slightest sound. Once I thought I heard something outside Tami's bedroom window and I got up and looked. It was a huge bird of some kind. I went back to bed and laid there thinking about the situation. Someone was looking for that lotto ticket but it didn't make sense to me. The police knew that the ticket had been sold to Mona. Anyone who turned it in now would be questioned about her death, and probably considered prime suspects. There was just something fishy about it that I couldn't quite get a grasp on yet.

It seemed to me that the house had been searched by someone who knew what they were doing. If I had searched it I probably would have been just as thorough although not as messy. There are ways to search thoroughly without leaving a sign that the place had been searched. It took a little more time to do it that way, but it could be done. The more I thought about it, the more convinced I became that whoever had searched the place knew that we would return in a short period of time.

Another thing that occurred to me was that the police had not been watching the place. A woman had been murdered. She had lived in the house for several years. A lotto ticket was missing that was a clue to who murdered the woman, and yet there were no police officers watching the residence. I spent several restless, sleepless minutes thinking about that.

By seven the next morning I had slept a total of maybe four hours. I felt as though I could sleep a week. The events of the past few days were hectic.

I got up and used the bathroom then went to the kitchen and put on a pot of coffee. I could hear Tami stirring in another part of the house. I was hoping that she wouldn't ask me to go to the funeral home with her. I don't like funeral homes, hospitals or cemeteries. My will states that when I kick out of this old world there will be no funeral, no "viewing" and no burial. Cremation and scattered ashes await me when it's my turn to go.

"Good morning," Tami said.

"Hi," I told her. "Are you up to the task in front of you today?"

"Not really," she said, dejectedly. "I know it is something I have to do, but I hate doing it. I might call and see if Gerri can go with me."

"That's a good idea," I said. I was thinking that I would go ask Happs why no one had been watching Tami's house.

"Can I fix you something to eat?" she asked.

"I'm going to fix you something," I told her. "Do you like oatmeal?"

"Yes," she said.

I got a box of Quaker Oats out of the cupboard and started preparing them for cooking in the microwave.

"What are you going to do today?" she asked.

"I'm going to talk to Detective Happs again," I said. "There are a few things I want to ask him. Then I'll go see the lotto commissioner and ask him a few more questions. That's in Tallahassee, so I may be gone a day or two. I'll ask Happs to keep a man over here while I'm gone. You should be OK."

"I'm not afraid," she said. "Whoever searched here probably will not be back."

I was thinking the same thing.

"Maybe you should spend a couple of days at Gerri's, if she won't mind."

"I'll ask her, Kip." Tami said. "I've spent a weekend with her before, I'm sure she won't mind, but really, I'll be OK here. I've got some more cleaning up to do."

We finished preparing breakfast and sat silently eating our oatmeal.

Another thing I was thinking about was trying to find the two goons who had picked a fight with me.

"Kip?"

"Yes."

"What is keeping you from just dumping all of my problems and continuing with your vacation? You don't have to help me."

"You asked for my help, Tami." I said, uncertain as to the direction this conversation was going.

"I mean, do you really want to help? Or are you just hanging around because you think you might have a chance to get me to go to bed with you?"

Nothing like being blunt, I thought.

She had touched a nerve, and I knew it. My emotions were hanging on my sleeves and I had on a short sleeve shirt.

"Tami, you're a beautiful girl. And I really think an awful lot of you. I'm attracted to you, both physically and emotionally. You and Mona were the nearest thing to a family setting I have had in years, since my divorce."

She gave me a look that told me I hadn't answered her question yet.

"I will help you." I said. "Whatever happens between us, we'll just wait and find out. I'm not going to lie to you, I find you very attractive sexually, and I'm feeling a little more than a sexual attraction. Why am I helping you?"

"Lets just say I hate people who take advantage of good decent folks. You and Mona deserve that money. You've worked hard all of your lives, you are honest, caring and trusting. I promise that when I find out who is responsible for Mona's death I'll get in my car and drive away, if that is what you want. If you want something different, I'll stay."

I sighed. That was more of an honest answer than I had given Rhonda when she asked me why I didn't want to marry her. My emotions were creeping up on me and I needed time to put all of that out of my head.

Tami sat eating her oatmeal, not saying a word. When she finished, she took her bowl to the sink cleaned it and put it on a drain board.

"You're the best thing that ever happened to me." She said.

CHAPTER FOURTEEN

Detective Happs wasn't unpleasant when I stopped by his office, but he seemed a little withdrawn, distant.

"Good morning, Mr. Yardley," he said.

"Detective Happs, thanks for seeing me." I said. "I just stopped by to see if you have any leads on the two kids that jumped me yesterday evening."

"I was going to call you about that," he said. He had my immediate attention. If he was going to call me, he must have something.

"We think the skinny one is Alberto Sarcosi," he said.

"Should that mean something to me?"

"I would suggest that you walk softly around Sarcosi for now, Yardley."

"Who is he?"

"It isn't so much him, it's who his father is." Happs said.

"OK," I said. "Who is his father?"

"Big Al Sarcosi," he said. "He's a minor player in the Miami mob. He owns a deli on South Dixie Highway. He can be a pretty tough cookie. We've kept a file on him for years. Suspected back in the old days of running a numbers racket, extortion, drugs, prostitution, you know, the shady side of life."

"And his son likes to pick on old guys?" I commented.

"The son tries to emulate the father," Happs told me. "We've picked him up for some minor infractions. The biggest rap we have on him is a hit and run where some old lady was killed. His old man bailed him and hired a mob lawyer. He went Scott free even though we had a lot on him."

"How do you think that happened?" I asked, although I had a pretty good hunch. Jury tampering, threats, bribery.

"A young prosecutor got cold feet," he said. "His case was a lot stronger than he presented in court."

"Bribery?"

"Probably just a threat," Happs told me. "The way things work in those circles is pretty scary. A guy gets in the way of the mob and goes home one night and finds a dead mackerel in his mailbox. No note, not anything we can trace, just a dead fish. He gets the hint and backs off."

"I don't scare easy," I told him.

"I figured that," he said. "That's why I suggested you walk softly. Whatever connection Sarcosi has with all of this is our job to discover, not yours. Let us handle it. If you go snooping around it might create more work for us. I'd hate to think California might lose one of their top private investigators here in Florida."

"Thanks for the compliment," I said. "And the warning. I'll watch my back."

"It's more than a warning, Yardley," he said, his face suddenly straighter. "I'm not asking you to back off, I'm telling you. You don't have a license here, and I don't want your blood on my hands."

"I see."

"I've ran a make on you, Yardley," he told me. "I know that you are considered one of the good guys out west. L.A. Police have you as a straight shooter, never crossing the lines like a lot of bad investigators, always keeping the departments involved in your cases. I expect the same courtesy here."

"I think they've over-rated me," I said. "And at the same time I think they have underestimated my determination. I don't back off, Happs. I don't have a license here, true. I am a U.S. citizen, however, and I have the constitutional right to go and come as I please. I also have the right of freedom of speech. I'll go where I want and ask the questions I need answers to. If I get any thing that I think you should know, you'll be the first one to hear about it."

"Walk softly, Yardley," he said, rose from his desk and opened his office door. I took the hint.

The first place I visited after leaving Happs office was the library. I wasn't sure, but I thought that Florida and California had a reciprocity agreement for private investigators doing business in their states. I looked it up. Happs had lied to me, either intentionally, to try to scare me, or not knowing the facts.

I didn't need a license in Florida. My California license gave me the right to investigate in Florida. While I was at the library I looked up Albert Sarcosi in the *Sun* records and found a small article about the hit and run trial. It seemed like Happs had given me the straight scoop on that.

I also found that Alberto Sarcosi, Senior, had been mentioned in a book by a local writer as having connections with the

New York mob. The author's name was Emory Letchman. I found the book with the aid of a cute librarian and sat back down to skim through it.

I was disappointed. The author had written about famous Mafia people who had lived or done business in Miami, with detailed stories about their lives, their business dealings and who they had influenced. The names Alberto Sarcosi and Carlos Fawn, however, were just listed in a chapter on "minor" members. No details. Just "believed to be connected to New York Mafia families."

I drove out south Dixie Highway and found the deli. I sat in the parking lot for twenty minutes watching the place, trying to get a feel of what I would say to either the young Sarcosi or his father. The place must have good food, a steady stream of customers went in. I noticed that of all the customers that went in, few came back out. Maybe there were tables and people were eating in.

I locked the dead stick on the Healey and went in. The room was bigger than I expected, but there were only 3 small tables, big enough for two people at each one. They were covered with the traditional red and white checked oilcloth table cloths. A small salad bar was on my left and a long glass deli counter at the back of the place ran nearly the full width of the room.

A dark skinned girl was at the counter. She asked me if she could help me in an accent I took to be Cuban. I asked to see Mr. Sarcosi. She left the counter and went to a room in the rear of the place, returning with a balding guy, heavy set, thick hairy arms and a tuft of black hair sticking out at the top of his shirt, around his neck.

"How can I help you?"

"Alberto Sarcosi?"

"That's a me," he said. "And who am I talking to?"

"My name is Kip Yardley," I told him. "Your son tried to pick a fight with me yesterday evening at a restaurant down south of Homestead." I watched his eyes. An immediate cloud of anger and hate emanated from them like death rays.

"You're the guy beat the hell out of my kid?"

"Your kid started the fracas," I told him. "I don't appreciate anyone insulting women, particularly women who are with me. But its more than that. I think he was sent to stall me while someone searched Mona Fawn's house."

I mentioned Mona's name to see what kind of reaction I would get from him. I saw nothing in his face.

"I ought to take your head off, Yardley," he said, stepping closer. I waited.

"Did you send him?" I asked.

"Send him? I don't know what the hell you're talking about. I didn't send anyone anywhere. Now get the hell out of my place before I take you apart."

I wasn't sure, but somehow I believed he was telling me the truth. At least about not sending anyone. I was ready if he tried to take me apart. He was younger than me, thirty pounds heavier with arms as big at the wrists as mine are at the bicep. Big men have never scared me, however. It's not how big a man is but how smart he is.

"Just a word of warning to you and your kid," I said. "Stay away from Tami Fawn."

I turned my back to him and walked towards the door.

"Hey!" I heard him yell. I stopped and turned slowly to face him.

"You want to hear about warnings? You ever lay a hand on my boy again, the sharks in Biscayne Bay will dine on your heart. You got that?"

"I guess we understand each other then," I told him. "Next time your boy comes near Tami Fawn, I'll cut off his salami and stick it up his ass."

I turned again. He yelled again. I turned back.

"You don't know who you are messing with. I got friends you don't even want to fool with. Guys with baseball bats that like busting kneecaps. A few with knives that like the sight of blood. If I want you gone, you'll go, and I can tell you it won't be pleasant. Now get the hell out of my deli and don't let me see you again."

I left.

CHAPTER FIFTEEN

It is a seven and a half hour drive from Miami to Tallahassee. I left at 5 the next morning, after spending a quiet evening with Tami at a movie and dinner. I drove the speed limit, letting the Healey out a couple of times just to pass slow moving trucks. The day was beautiful, Florida sunshine warmed my face and bare arms as I enjoyed the ride. I had a few things on my mind. First one was why someone would search Tami's house for a lotto ticket when the cops knew that the purchaser was murdered?

I found the Lotto Commissioner's office without difficulty using my GPS system. I call the system "Annie" and I talk to it. I know that sounds stupid, but then all new electronic modern devices create stupidity. I've never figured out why people text someone on a cell phone when they could just as easily talk to them.

Oliver La Fleur's secretary was a very nice looking blond. She batted her eyelids at me as I entered his office and smiled.

"Good afternoon, Sir," she said. "May I help you?" Her voice was high pitched, she sounded like a teenaged boy who's voice hadn't changed yet.

"I would like to speak to Mr. La Fleur," I told her.

"Do you have an appointment?"

"I didn't know I would need one," I said. "It's about a murder down in Homestead."

Her eyes got wide and she stared at me. "Murder?"

"Yeah, you know, when somebody cuts someone else's throat, that is usually called murder, unless it's done on an operating table then it's called surgery."

"You want to talk about a murder?"

"What part of murder do you not understand?" I asked. "I'd like to speak to Mr. La Fleur now. May I go in?"

"Mr. La Fleur doesn't see anyone without an appointment," she said, shaking her head and trying to regain her composure.

I looked at my watch. It was 12:45.

"Get him on the intercom and make an appointment for me," I said. "I'll wait, beautiful."

She looked pleased. Then she looked me up and down from the dark hair with gray temples, all the way down my body, past the white tee shirt I wore that advertised a Southern California golf course, past the dark blue Chinos to the white tennis shoes.

I'm not sure what she was thinking, but the word beautiful works miracles sometimes when you need a woman to do something for you. She complied with my request.

"Mr. La Fleur, there's a gentleman here who wants to speak to you about a murder."

"What?" I heard him yell through the wires.

"A murder, Sir," she said. "Down by Homestead."

"Homestead? Ask him if his name is Yardley."

"Are you Mister Yardley?"

"That's me," I said.

"That's him," she said.

"Send him in," he said.

I went in. La Fleur was a jolly fat man. He was big. Six feet tall and in the neighborhood of three hundred pounds. He scooted his chair back from his desk as I entered his plush office.

"Keep your seat," I said. "I won't take much of your time."

"You drove all the way from Homestead to see me, Yardley," he said. "I've got plenty of time. Now what is it you want?"

"It occurred to me that someone who finds a lotto ticket purchased by someone else could cash that ticket in, but would they?"

"Meaning?"

"Well, lets say I bought a lotto ticket and the press reported that I had bought the ticket, then I lost it. Would whoever found it be able to cash it? The press has already said that I bought it, so wouldn't that make the ticket mine?"

"I see what your getting at," he said, running his fingers through his thinning gray hair.

"You mean the ticket that Mona Fawn bought is not any good to anyone else since the police know she bought it and that someone murdered her."

"Well, yeah. That's what I mean," I said. "But wouldn't the scenario I described be true also?"

"Not necessarily," he said. "If someone buys a ticket and dies, the ticket becomes the property of that party's estate, and the estate can collect the prize money."

"So Tami could claim the prize if she finds the ticket?"

"Absolutely. She is the daughter of the winner, thus she would be entitled to the winner's estate which includes the ticket."

"What about someone else finding it and trying to cash it?"

"In Florida, a lotto ticket is considered a "bearer" instrument. Anyone who presents the ticket to this office would be entitled to the prize. They would not have to prove that they purchased it," he told me. "That is why we recommend that anyone who wins the lotto immediately sign the ticket in the space provided on the back. That signature must match the bearer's signature when a ticket is presented for payment."

"That brings me to the point I wanted to ask you about," I said. "If the ticket is never found, what happens to the money?"

"About sixty percent of the money goes to the Education Fund, twenty percent goes to the kitty for the next lotto drawing."

"That's eighty percent," I said. "What about the other twenty percent?"

"That's money that the Lotto Commission uses to run the games," he said. "It takes a lot of money to provide the tickets, pay the distributors, do advertising and promotions."

"And that budget is under your office?" I asked.

"Yes it is, Yardley. I would be the one who would sign any checks for money drawn from that account."

I sat there for a moment, not saying anything, just letting the wheels in my brain turn slowly.

"Did I answer your questions?" he asked.

"Yes, Mr. La Fleur," I said. "Thank you for your time."

As I left his office there was one thing that kept clanging away like a bell in my old gray matter. Mona Fawn may have not been killed for the lotto ticket. She may have been killed to prevent her from cashing the lotto ticket. If someone tried to steal the ticket but couldn't find it, wouldn't they want Mona to live long enough to lead them to it?

But who would have anything to gain if the ticket was never redeemed? It appeared at this point that the State of Florida would be the big winner, particularly the education system.

I walked the short distance to the parking lot where I had left the Healey. When I got to the car my heart danged near stopped in my chest.

All four tires were flat. The dead stick was still firmly attached to brake and steering wheel. In the drivers side seat was a rolled up newspaper. In the newspaper was a dead mackerel.

CHAPTER SIXTEEN

At the sight of the four flat tires, I was scared. *At the sight of the newspaper with the dead mackerel rolled inside, I was angry.* I used my cell phone to call the auto club and then I called Tallahassee police. They arrived at the parking lot in minutes. While I was talking to the officer the auto club showed up and the guy explained that he couldn't fix the flats because all four valve stems had been cut off. They would have to tow the car to a repair station.

The police officer took my report. I left out the part about the dead mackerel. That was my personal information. When I find the guy that left it, I intend to do some serious bodily harm. The police didn't need to know in advance that I intend to break someone's arms and legs. The officer advised me to keep closer watch on my vehicle, explaining that it was a high theft item and it might disappear never to be seen again in America.

I asked the auto club driver if I could ride with him to the repair place and he agreed. I climbed in the cab of his truck and waited while they loaded the Healey on a flat bed ramp truck.

Less than two miles away the truck pulled into a Michelin tire shop and they had it fixed in an hour. I had time to think about the incident a little more. I knew that the Healey might wind up stolen, burned to a crisp, or even smashed up. That made me think of the night the two kids had picked a fight; the incident when someone had nearly T-boned us while Tami was driving to the Mexican restaurant. Time to hide the Healey, I thought.

I paid the tire shop guy and ran my card through the auto club's scanner. I walked back to the guy's truck with him and when I had him out of earshot of the tire shop I slipped him a twenty and asked him a question.

"Is there a storage place where I can leave my car, one that is secure and guarded 24-7?"

He gave me the address of a place. He assured me that it was as secure as you could find. Chain link fence around the units, guard on duty 24-7. Licensed, insured and even patrolled by the Tallahassee police.

I found the place without difficulty, paid in advance for a month's rent, locked the dead stick on the Healey and left it in a 8 x 10 unit with steel doors and double padlocks. I used my cell phone and called a cab and had it take me to the Tallahassee airport. There I rented a late model Lincoln and headed back south towards Homestead.

Someone had followed me to Tallahassee. I didn't think they could pick up my trail from the airport back to Homestead, but just in case, I got off the interstate a few times, did some rear view mirror checking, and after a few twists and turns, got back on the highway south.

When I reached Miami it was nearly midnight. I stopped at a drugstore and purchased a pair of rubber gloves, then I drove the big Lincoln out on Dixie Highway to the deli owned by Alberto Sarcosi. The lights were out, the parking lot was empty. I sat in the Lincoln for a few minutes watching the front of the place. There wasn't any activity. I put the gloves on.

I walked quickly to the front door and used a set of picks and a credit card to open it. Once inside I made my way to the back and took a knife from a block holder near the meat counter. In Sarcosi's office, I took a framed picture from his desk. It was a picture of Alberto, two teen aged kids, a boy and a girl, and a woman I took to be his wife.

I took the back off of the frame and extracted the picture. I tore out the woman and the girl, leaving Sarcosi senior and junior. I laid the newspaper with the mackerel on Sarcosi's desk, laid the picture of the two males on top of it and I drove the knife through the picture, through the newspaper and mackerel, and a half an inch or so into the shiny maple top of Sarcosi's desk.

Then I left.

CHAPTER SEVENTEEN

I slept fitfully in the motel room. Each time I drifted off to sleep I saw the Austin Healey with 4 flat tires and it seemed as though I could smell rotting Mackerel. I would wake up breathing deeply, wide awake. I would sit on the edge of the bed for a long time, thinking. Maybe I shouldn't have been so revengeful in my reaction to Sarcosi's show of power. It just irked me though to think that a low-life scum like Alfredo Sarcosi, Jr. could get away with things just because his daddy had connections with the mob. It really ticked me off that someone had attacked a valued possession like my Austin Healey, to get at me.

I finally drifted off to sleep and woke up at 6 the following morning, wondering how long it would take for Sarcosi to react to my response to his act. Would I find the Lincoln that I had rented rigged with a stick of dynamite to blow as soon as I turned the key? I wondered about it, but I didn't worry about it. I've lived through some actions that would make most people cringe, and went on with life. If you live in fear, you'll die afraid. I planned on dying with my boots off and in the company of a beautiful young lady, not shivering in a motel room afraid of the Mafia, or a bunch of wannabee punks.

I showered and dressed and watched TV for an hour then left, found a Cracker Barrel restaurant and had breakfast and pondered what my next course of action would be. Tami wouldn't be at home, I knew. I would have to get in touch with her and find out about the funeral for Mona, but I hadn't taken the time or opportunity to get her cell phone number.

I called the hospital where she worked and talked to a friendly operator, gave her my cell number and asked her to get a message to Tami to call me. The library seemed like a good place to kill some time while waiting for her call, so I drove back to the same one I had visited. I didn't know what I wanted to research, I just needed to kill some time, but soon found myself on a computer looking at the Miami-Dade County school district. There were a couple of things that I was kicking around in the old gray matter. One was the reason why Mona Fawn was unable to read and write even though she had completed 10 years of school.

The other was who was in charge of the money that the school district would get as a result of the $114 million dollar lotto ticket *not* being cashed.

I came up with a name. William Stevens. School board chairman. Real Estate developer. He was worth several million dollars, had ties with Miami-Dade County politics, and might be the place for me to start asking questions. I called the school board office. The phone rang several times which was puzzling to me until I realized that it was Saturday.

I left the library, not really knowing what my next move would be. There wasn't any point in making any contact with the Sarcosis, I'd probably just stir up a bigger hornet's nest if I did. I got in the Lincoln and sat thinking about things. One of the items that kept coming back to me was the death of Mona's parents in an airplane crash in Georgia. I wondered if ValJean DuPont knew Mona's parents. He said he had known her in school, maybe he could shed some light on how her parents died. I started the big Lincoln and headed out towards the coast

wondering if I could find my way back to
ValJean's strange boat-raft home.

It didn't take me long to drive back to
the marina and find the odd shaped boat that
ValJean DuPont called home. I parked the
Lincoln in the lot and walked to the ramp
that stretched 50 feet out to the dock where
the floating home gently moved up and down.
I knocked on the door and waited.

ValJean opened the door dressed in a
pair of shorts and no shirt. His hairy chest
was damp with perspiration and he hadn't
shaved in a couple of days. I could smell a
sour odor that I recognized as a bad
hangover. Val had been drinking too much
of his home-made rum.

"Oh, hello Rudyard Kipling Yardley,"
he said.

I was amazed that he had remembered
my full name.

"ValJean DuPont," I said. "Did I catch
you at a bad time?"

"Nah, come in, I'm just trying to fix my
air conditioner, the damned thing went out
on me."

He held the door open and I walked
into the one room interior of his boat. It was

hot inside. He came in and left the door open.

"Cooler outside than it is inside," he murmured. "What brings you out my way, Kip? And where's that beautiful Austin Healey?"

"I just have a couple of questions I wanted to ask you about the Fawn family," I said. "The Healey is locked up in storage up in Tallahassee. I'm driving a rented car."

"Why?"

"Someone cut all four valve stems."

"What in the world would anyone do that for?" he asked.

"As a warning to me, I guess."

"Warning for what?"

"I had a run in with a punk named Alfred Sarcosi," I waited, watching his eyes to see if there was any recognition in them. I thought I saw a little widening and slight uplift of his eyebrows.

"Does that name ring a bell?" I asked.

"I know a guy named Sarcosi," he said. "He runs a deli out on the highway."

"That's him," I said. "Or rather that is the punk's old man. I had some words with him. He doesn't like me very much. I think it was the senior Sarcosi that had someone follow me to Tallahassee and flatten my tires."

"Sounds like something he would do," ValJean said. He scratched his hairy chest and walked stiffly towards a small air conditioning unit on the far wall from the door.

"This damned thing is drawing too much current," he said. "Where the hell is my volt-amp meter, I just had the damned thing."

He turned to face me looking left and right and then looked directly at me.

"I'm sorry, Kip," he said. "I should have offered you a drink. I'm fresh out, though. Say, I wonder if you could loan me a twenty? I've got to buy some wire to fix this air conditioner and I won't get my check until next week."

I fished out my wallet and opened it, peeled two twenties out and handed them to him. I said, "I don't need a drink. Just some information I thought you might have."

"Lets go outside," he said. "It's too damned hot in here." He stuffed the two twenties into his shorts pocket.

He walked out the open door and I followed. A cool breeze was drifting in from the bay and I was glad to get out of the stuffy boat. Not only was it hot but it had the odor of a sweaty alcoholic, the bed was unmade, and the sink was full of dirty dishes.

"What kind of information do you think I might know?"

"Did you know Mona's grandfather?" I asked.

"Carlos?" he asked.

"Yes."

"Well I can't say I knew him real well. He worked construction for the railroad and was involved in the union."

"What did he do for the railroad?"

"Bricklayer, I think," he said. "There used to be a repair station in Homestead years ago. I remember a big building out towards the old airport where the tracks ran back in those days. There was a siding to take engines in to the building. I think Carlos built it."

"What was Carlos's connection with the mob?"

"You mean the Mafia? He was a union leader, that's all I know. The Mafia had a lot of influence with the union. You couldn't move anything without them knowing about it."

"How old was Carlos when he died?" I asked.

"Not old enough," was his cryptic reply.

"What?"

"He didn't live his life out," ValJean said, looking out across the bay.

"He died young?"

"You could say that," he glanced at me, then back out across the bay.

"Heart attack?"

"No, probably shot."

"What?"

He wiped his brow with a dirty handkerchief and looked at me. "Carlos disappeared right after the funeral for Harry and his wife."

"Disappeared?"

"He just disappeared."

"But I thought Mona was raised by her grandfather."

"People have two grandfathers, Kip."

"Oh. It was Hannah's father that raised Mona?"

"Yeah."

"What was his name?"

"I figured you would have found that by now," he said. "You found Hannah D. Fawn didn't you?"

"Yeah. Harry's wife. She died in the airplane crash with him."

"She was Hannah DuPont before she married Harry."

"I found an article in the library that said Mona was in the custody of Carlos after her parents died," I said.

"For about two weeks." He scratched his chin, wiped the sweat off of his forehead again. "Then Charles and Meredith DuPont filed for custody and the court granted it. The grounds they used was the book by Emory Lechman that said Carlos was a minor member of the mob."

"DuPont?" I asked. "Relation to you?"

"Say, Kip, do you mind if I go down to the store and get some wire. I've got to get this air conditioner fixed."

I looked at him and saw that all of the sweating he was doing was a definite sign that he was waiting to get his hands on something to drink. I almost regretted giving him the two twenties, but then he had given me some more information to check, and I felt that something that he had told me was important, but I just couldn't define its importance or remember what it was. Old age creeps up on us all. Someday soon I am going to have to give up this PI business and go fishing. That is if I can remember how to bait a hook.

CHAPTER EIGHTEEN

The funeral for Mona Fawn was on Monday. I attended and sat near the back of the chapel at the funeral home. When it was over an attendant started motioning people to get up and go towards the front, to pass by the casket and say their final goodbyes.

I didn't want to see Mona lying in a casket. Maybe I'm funny that way, but I wanted to remember her dancing around the kitchen of her home, lithe and living and beautiful. Tami was in the front row along with some people I didn't know. Must be from the DuPont family, I thought.

I followed the hearse to a cemetery and stood watching as the people stood around the grave site, solemn and quiet. I couldn't hear the words being spoken by the preacher. It didn't matter. No amount of words would ever take the place of the night Tami and Mona had planned how to spend their fortune. They finished the ceremony and the preacher plucked red roses from a wreath that lay on top of the casket and gave them to the family.

Tami was beautiful, even in the blackest summer dress I had ever seen. Her lips quivered a few times and I could see a tear, like a pearl, escape from her eye and slide gently down over the olive cheeks and drop silently to the ground. When it was over, I waited near the rented Lincoln and watched as the family members were loaded into white limos and ushered back to the funeral home. I followed.

That afternoon there was the traditional meal served at Tami's home. Fried chicken and cold cuts and potato salad, wine in bottles wrapped with black dinner napkins. I stayed in the background, trying hard to be inconspicuous but nodding politely when Tami introduced me to various members of the family, cousins and friends.

One man was of particular interest to me. It was Charles DuPont. He was probably nearing ninety years of age, but walked with a steady gate and ate his meal with untrembling hands. His snow white hair was full and combed straight back, neatly cut. He wore a dark blue suit and a silky not so dark blue shirt with a plain tie. His bearing and dress showed that he was used to the finer things of life. Tami introduced me to him and I shook his hand. His grip was firm, not strong, as he looked directly into my eyes.

"Tami tells me that you have agreed to conduct your own investigation in regards to Mona's death, Mr. Yardley?"

"Yes, Sir," I said. "Please, call me Kip."

"Do you have credentials, Kip?" he asked. "I'm not trying to be rude, but there are so many crooks in today's society that might want to play games with Tami's emotions, in her grief."

It occurred to me that Charles DuPont was the first person I had met and talked to regarding Mona's death that had asked to see my credentials. I will flash my California PI license on occasion if it will help me to get an answer from someone who is hesitant to talk to a stranger, but Charles was cautious enough to want to make sure that I was indeed on Tami's side.

I pulled out my wallet and opened it, showing him my license and my drivers license from California.

"Oh, a California investigator?"

"Yes, Sir."

"Well, that's proof enough for me, Kip. I hope you find the person behind this terrible tragedy. Mona was my only granddaughter. My wife and I raised her after her parents were killed."

"I have been told that," I said, folding my wallet and putting it back in my pocket.

"By whom?"

His question caught me off guard. Tami had not told me, I had learned that bit of information from ValJean.

"A friend that I met recently told me that, Sir."

"And your friend's name?"

I wondered why this was important to him, but I saw no reason not to tell him.

"ValJean DuPont," I said.

His eyes narrowed a little and he gave me an odd look.

"I see," he told me.

It suddenly occurred to me that I had not seen ValJean DuPont at the funeral, the graveside or here at the meal in Tami's home. Maybe he was hung over and just couldn't get sober enough to make it, or maybe he was too busy fixing the air conditioner on his strange floating home.

"The strange ValJean," he said. "You will be well advised to take anything that ValJean tells you with an ample grain of salt, Kip." He looked away, as if that was his final word on the subject. I didn't pursue that, instead I excused myself and went outside, talked to a few people who were milling around in the yard, smoking cigarettes and talking quietly. One of the women approached me and I recognized Gerri, the nurse from the hospital, and Tami's friend.

"Hello Mr. Yardley," she said.

"Hello, Gerri," I smiled and shook her hand gently.

"I'm so glad that you are helping Tami," she told me. "That poor girl has had a really tough life, and now losing her mother like this is about all any girl can take. It's nice to know that she has a friend like you. And a handsome friend at that."

I shifted from one foot to the other, not replying. It always embarrasses me when someone calls me "handsome" or "good looking". At the same time, I was curious as to what Tami and Gerri had talked about in regards to my relationship with Tami. I didn't dare ask, though. It would have been impolite to ask that question in the best of times, but downright dumb to ask it here at Mona's wake.

Gerri smiled at me. "Take good care of her, Kip. She's a sweetheart and she means a lot to my husband and me."

She walked away and I found myself ambling towards the house, meaning to go and get another glass of wine.

Tami met me at the door and took my hand. She led me back out into the yard, away from the smokers.

"Can we go somewhere after everyone leaves?" she asked.

"Sure, Tami," I said. "Where would you like to go?"

"Anywhere but here," she said. "I just want to get away from people for awhile. Maybe just go for a drive down by the beach where we met?"

"Sure," I said. "Let me know when you want to get away, maybe I can spread the word to the people here that the host would like to be alone."

"No," she said. "Don't say anything, they'll all be leaving soon enough."

And she was right. Within an hour the last of the friends and relatives of Mona Fawn had left.

Charles DuPont shook my hand when he left and gave me an impressive looking business card along with a firm handshake.

"When you find time, please stop by and see me, Mr. Yardley," he said. "I have some things I'd like to tell you in private that might be of value to you."

That piqued my curiosity.

CHAPTER NINETEEN

I was still relaxing outside the house in a chaise lounge after all the guests had left and Tami was inside. I thought that I would give her time to herself to grieve privately now that the wake was over. I was starting to doze off to sleep when I heard my name.

"Kip," she called.

I got up and walked towards the door. She stood there in a pair of jeans and halter, her black hair loose around her shoulders, no make-up, lovely as a sunrise.

"Do you want to go now?" I asked.

"Yes," she said. "Do you want anything before we go? Another glass of wine?"

"No," I told her. "I'll drive. We can take some wine with us if you'd like.'

"OK" she said and retreated into the house. I followed.

She walked ahead of me into the kitchen and opened a cupboard. She picked a bottle of wine, Sauvignon Blanc, a light color, distinctive aroma and herb like taste, one of my favorites.

It was a mild day, the mid afternoon sun winked in and out between fluffy clouds that drifted in from the Atlantic. I drove by my motel room and changed into shorts and tee shirt. It didn't take us long to drive to the parking lot near the beach where we had met. Tami carried the wine in a plastic bag, along with two plastic wine glasses and she took my hand as we walked across the sand towards the waters edge. The beach was nearly deserted, only a family of four, mother, father and two small children, sat near us.

We spread a blanket and sat down on it, Tami removed her jeans and halter to reveal the perfect body in a pink bikini. I took off my tee shirt.

We sat talking quietly for several minutes, sipping the sweet wine and watching the children play in the edge of the water.

"I would have given them the lotto ticket," she said suddenly. "They didn't have to kill Mona."

I remained silent. It's difficult to think of something to say when you know the party you are with is suffering from grief. I put my hand over hers but didn't speak.

"I'm sorry, Kip." she said. "I just can't help thinking about why someone would want to kill Mona. I'm sure that she would have given them the ticket to save her life. I sometimes think that there must have been a different reason."

I couldn't remain silent any longer. She had voiced an opinion that had lingered near the surface of my mind all during the funeral service.

"Was there any indication in the last few months that Mona was frightened of something? Do you know of any arguments or anything remotely near a reason someone might not want Mona around any longer?"

"I've racked my brain," she said. "I can't think of anything."

We sat there silently, Tami looked away from me and I knew there were tears in her eyes.

"There's something I need to ask you," I said. "You told me the day we met that you had to write a letter for Mona. You've never told me why Mona could not write the letter herself, and I know that she was president of her class when she was a sophomore. What happened to make her unable to write?"

"She suffered from a psychological block," Tami told me. "When Grandfather Harry and Grandmother Hannah were killed, Mona went into a deep depression. Part of that depression, and perhaps the medication doctors gave her to overcome it, caused a mental regression. Mentally she reverted back to a child. Oh, she could function as an adult, drive a car, cook, clean house, buy groceries, understand conversations and television programs, but she could not read or write. Whatever psychological impairment she had refused to let her mind function past the level of a five year old when it came to reading and writing. Doctors could not figure it out."

"Did Mona go to counseling recently?"

"Yes, it was a continuing counseling process," Tami said. "She had been going to a psychologist since the accident, and had been functioning on a perfectly normal basis except for reading and writing."

"Would you mind giving me the name of the psychologist she was seeing?"

"Doctor Roflecion, a prominent Miami psychologist."

"Did you go with her?"

"No, I couldn't," she said. "Mona didn't want me to go with her, she preferred going alone. And, too, my job hours were not conducive to attending Mona's sessions."

"You do know where she was going, and who she was seeing?"

"Oh yes," she turned to face me. "I've been pretty much Mona's caretaker in that respect. I've taken care of nearly all the business transactions and accounting functions in her life since I was in my teens."

"Who did that for her before you took on the responsibility?"

"Grandfather DuPont." Tami said.

"Mona's grandfather?"

"Yes, you met him today."

"He said he wanted me to stop and visit with him. He said he had some things to tell me."

"Are you going to?"

"Do you think I shouldn't?"

"I didn't mean it that way," she said. "I have no idea what Grandfather has that you might need to know. Surely he feels that whatever he has to tell you is important enough for you to hear."

"Then I'll go see him." I said.

Tami remained silent and I took that as a notion that I should also refrain from commenting further on the subject.

She looked at me for a moment then turned her body on the blanket so that she was facing me. She put one leg on one side of me and the other leg on the other side, then extended her arms, taking my hands in hers. I sat there looking into her dark eyes. I could feel the tension in her hands and heart. As we looked at each other, the tension seemed to vanish, like turning a switch and dimming a light.

I felt a tug on my hands, a gentle pulling motion. I leaned forward until my face was inches from hers. She let go of my hands and wrapped hers behind my neck, very slowly and gently pulling my face closer.

I kissed her. The kiss was emotional and exciting. I was captured by her beauty and the warmth of her body. She let her body fall backwards, pulling me down on her. My bare chest was pressed against her upper body.

"Kip," she said, softly.

"Yes?"

"If I find the ticket, will you share the luxury with me?"

"Would you want me to?"

"I want you to be a part of my life," she said.

I kissed her again.

We lay in each others arms, kissing occasionally, not speaking. The sun crept lower towards the horizon behind the city. The young couple and their children left the beach. The breeze stopped and sounds became soft and muted. The gentle slap of water on the sand was mesmerizing.

After a while we left.

CHAPTER TWENTY

I slept late the next morning. After taking Tami home from the beach, I drove back to the motel room and finished the bottle of wine we had taken with us, took a shower and went to bed. I felt more tired than I had in months. It was almost as if I was coming down with the flu or something, my body was just simply tired. I made a mental note to go in for a physical when this ordeal was over and I got back to California.

Then I realized why I was tired. It was a mental thing, not physical. I was torn between to wants. The want to stay with Tami and the want to go back to Rhonda. The part of me that wanted to go back was losing. I wasn't sure I wanted it to lose.

I lay awake for a long time thinking. I tried to put the mystery of the lotto ticket and Mona's death out of my mind and concentrate on the choices I felt I would soon have to make. All of my training in martial arts about blanking my mind and meditation and focus failed to help. My heart was screaming out to me to help Tami find Mona's killer.

I finally drifted off to sleep.

At eight the next morning I woke up. I had turned the air conditioner off in the room before going to bed and now the room was warm. I was sweating, the wine I had finished had dehydrated me. I was thirsty, hot and still felt tired, although I had slept more than 8 hours.

I showered and shaved and got dressed. It was nearly ten by the time I had eaten breakfast in the motel's dining room and I was beginning to feel better. There were no pressing clues that jumped out at me about Mona and the lotto ticket so I decided I would visit Charles DuPont. I got the card he had given me, punched in his number on my cell phone and waited as it buzzed.

Whoever it was that answered put me on hold after telling me that "Mr. DuPont was expecting my call."

"Charles," he said, as an introduction when he came on the line.

"Good morning, Sir," I said. "This is Kip Yardley. You suggested that I stop in to see you, is this morning convenient?"

"Oh, hello, Kip," he said. "Yes, I have some time at about eleven. Do you know how to find my home?"

"I have a GPS if you'll give me your address I'm sure I can find it," I said.

He rattled off the street address. I jotted it down on the back of his card. Fourteen Hialeah Park Drive. We said our goodbyes and I programmed the GPS that had came with the car rental.

It turned out to be the upper crust side of Miami. Homes in the neighborhood looked like some of the homes I had seen in Beverly Hills back in California. Most were stucco mansions. I knew that the stucco covered concrete blocks were probably reinforced with steel here in Florida. In California the homes would have been stucco covering chicken wire and wood frames. The difference in potential disasters, I thought. Earthquakes versus hurricanes.

The DuPont estate was surrounded by a stucco covered wall, eight feet high. The entrance was through electronically controlled gates of wrought iron. As I drove near the gates opened. I saw pink flamingos on the lawn and thought how tacky to have those plastic pink flamingos in a luxury home. Then I realized that they were real flamingos. Spread across the immense lawn were little mini-ponds, two feet or so deep, with water fountains spraying plumes of water up ten feet into the air and tinkling back into the pools.

Palm trees were everywhere there wasn't a pond. Lush grass grew around the trees. A lawns keeper's nightmare, I thought. How do they cut the grass and keep it out of the ponds?

The cobblestone driveway curved it's way through five acres of grass and lawns, manicured as if they had been cut with a nail clipper. The flamingos paid little attention to the Lincoln, occasionally shifting legs as I drove through.

So Mona was not raised in abject poverty, I was thinking, as I stopped the Lincoln at the end of the drive where it made a loop. I got out and walked the remaining fifteen yards to the low step that took me to an entry way.

A massive oak double door, arched at the top, faced me. I pushed a lighted button on the right of the door and heard chimes echo through the house.

Moments later a small, dark-skinned man opened the door.

"Mr. Yardley?" he asked in an accent I took to be Philippine.

"Yes," I said.

"My name is Juan," he told me, smiling. "Mr. DuPont is expecting you. Right this way, please."

I followed him through a maze of doors and rooms, some of them as big as tennis courts. We arrived at a room somewhere at the back of the house, a huge room at one end of an open kitchen. There were screens across the back and outside was a sparkling swimming pool big enough to float the Queen Mary. If DuPont had invited me here to impress me, he was succeeding. The place must be worth several million.

He was seated at a small table, a colorful looking drink sat in front of him.

"Good morning, Kip," he said, rising.

"Good morning, Sir," I said.

"Please, call me Charles," he told me. "I'm not used to formality."

He motioned to the small man. "Juan, get Mr. Yardley a drink."

Then to me, "Coffee? A cocktail?"

"I'll have whatever that is you are drinking," I said, pointing to the colorful drink.

"Ah, it's a Tequila Sunrise. Fix Mr. Yardley a Tequila Sunrise, Juan. Please, have a seat." He motioned for me to sit down. Juan pulled a chair out for me. After I was seated he seemed to disappear.

"Thank you, Charles." I said. "I'm curious as to what you wanted to tell me."

"First, let me ask you something," he said. "If you don't mind."

"Not at all," I said.

"When do you plan to return to your home state of California, and your agency there?"

"I'm not sure," I said, honestly. It was a curious question. He knew that I was trying to help Tami.

"I see," he said.

"If you are asking how long will it take to find Mona's killer, the answer is still the same, I'm not sure. Whatever time it takes, I'll stay. When I find some answers, I'll make a decision as to my returning home."

"I understand," he said. "Do you have anything that you think might be leading you towards your goal?"

It was apparent that he didn't like saying the words, "Mona's killers". I noticed that his eyes became a little watery when I mentioned Mona.

"I've really just started asking some questions," I said. For some reason my mind was sending me a mixed message. I could hear the little subconscious voice telling me to find out what he wanted to tell me and keep what I knew under my hat.

"I understand you have made an enemy." he said.

I was suddenly alert. If he had a source that knew about Alfredo Sarcosi, and my run-in with the two punks, maybe he had sources that could tell me more.

"I'm not sure I know what you are referring to." I said.

"Let's not be coy with each other," he said, staring at me with the pale blue eyes that seemed to look right into my soul.

"I make enemies wherever I go," I said. "It comes with the job. Someone gets killed, I try to find out who killed them. I ask questions, some people are offended by my questions. Either that or they just do not like answering questions. If I step on someone's toes, that's part of the game."

"Don't play Mike Hammer with me, Kip."

"What does that mean?" I asked, even though I knew the answer. My tough guy approach with Mr. DuPont was not going to work. He saw through it too soon.

"I've been in public relations for almost seventy years. All that you see here is the result of being astute enough to keep my feelers out and my feelings hidden. It's an intuition that has served me well. There is little you can do that will remain unknown to me. I have friends all over this state that will tell me every move you make. I know about your visit to Sarcosi."

"Oh that," I said, trying hard not to sound jaded.

"You may need my help when it comes to dealing with Sarcosi," he said.

"How can you help? The man is a bully. He may have ties with the big boys, but one on one he doesn't scare me. I've learned that if you let fear control your life you might as well crawl into an early grave and pull the dirt in on top of you."

"I agree." He said. "But to purposefully agitate an alligator while you are in the swamp is not too smart. There's an old saying, 'It's hard to remember that your objective is to drain the swamp when you are up to your ass in alligators.' Does that make sense to you?"

"Yes it does." I said. "At the same time, I am a student of animal behavior. I know that the moment a wild animal senses that you fear it, it will be twice as dangerous. I know that it is wise and cautious to be wary, but it can be just as wise and cautious to let your enemy know that you do not fear them. As Churchill said, 'all we have to fear is fear itself'. Does that make sense to you, Mr. DuPont?"

He looked at me for several seconds. I thought I read something in his eyes that told me his respect for me had gone up a few notches. When he spoke, I wasn't sure.

"I am not the enemy," he said. "I just want to make sure that you know what you are dealing with. There are just as many people in my circle of informers that are not on my side, or yours. There are people who know what you had for breakfast this morning. There are people who would have put arsenic in whatever you had for breakfast for less than a thousand dollars. To stir the hornet's nest is to invite the stings. I'm just asking you to be careful. I want to find out who killed Mona as much as you do. Please watch your step."

"Is that why you wanted me to stop by? If that is all you wanted to tell me, you've wasted my time."

"Don't be hasty," he said. "I don't know everything that you have learned. If you will fill me in, maybe I can think of an avenue you haven't explored."

"What do you want me to tell you? I've just started this investigation. I don't really know a whole lot about anything yet."

"Please. Tell me what you have done. If I find that there is something you do not know, a piece of information I can give you, I'll tell you. Remember, I'm the one with sources of information. I may have already discovered something that will assist your investigation."

"I'm too old to go through the legwork, but I'm not too old to keep my ears open and my strings out. On top of that, I have accumulated a little wealth through the years. Money is a great persuader, Kip. The word is already out on the street that certain pieces of information may be worth certain dollar amounts. I'm not saying that your detective agency is not doing well, financially, but I don't think you can match me, dollar for dollar, as to what I am willing to pay for a lead that will give me Mona's killer."

I thought about that for a while. He was right. As much as I hated to think about it, he was absolutely right. He could be a big asset. In the back of my mind, however, I was thinking that if the information he could buy wasn't what he wanted to hear, he might be a liability just as easily.

"OK. I'll tell you what I know." I said, picked up my drink and took a sip.

I started with the library. I told him what I knew about his son-in-law, the airplane crash that had taken his daughter's life, the background investigation that Happs had done on Mona, the hassle with the kids at the Mexican restaurant, the search of Mona's home. I told him everything that I thought might have a bearing on which way I would go next. The problem was, I didn't have a clue as to which way I would go.

In the cobwebs of my brain I was beginning to see a connection with some unsavory characters known commonly as "The Mob". How I was going to pursue that line of questioning was still in doubt.

When I finished I took another sip of the drink and set it down.

"That's all I've got," I said. "Can you add to that?"

"I just have a few things," he said. "First, I think you should forget about the lotto ticket, don't let that be your reason for taking this investigation. If you find it, none of the money is yours. You will be paid, of course, by me, if you find Mona's killers. The lotto ticket belongs to Tami. And as my great granddaughter, you must know that Tami will be provided for, the lotto ticket is not her salvation."

I started to say something but he interrupted.

"The part of the investigation that concerns me goes deeper than Mona's death. I want to know who killed my son-in-law and daughter."

My attention was immediately diverted to that subject. To the limits of my knowledge, the airplane crash that had killed Mona's father and mother was an accident. His words made it immediately different in my mind. It was an avenue I had not discovered or explored.

"You think that it wasn't just an accident?"

"I've spent a lot of money trying to buy information regarding that "accident", Kip. It was money wasted until a few months ago. Then I got word that there was a mechanical gadget found in the wreckage that didn't belong there. It was not standard equipment on that type of aircraft, in fact, the accident investigators didn't think it was a part of the aircraft. That's why it was never reported by anyone. My source thought different."

"It was a fuel shut off switch, designed to be activated by remote control. Whoever put that switch between the aircraft's fuel tank and the engine must have had some knowledge of mechanics and electronics. Someone on the ground simply pushed a button, the fuel stopped flowing and the aircraft fell from the sky."

"Remote controlled?" I said.

"Yes. Like in model airplane remote controls. I'm sure you are familiar with the flying models that people buy and fly on Sunday afternoons at parks and in their own club spaces. There are several model aircraft flying clubs around Miami."

"I see," I said. And I was beginning to see. Someone had not wanted Mona's parents to return from New York. They had waited in the mountains under the flight pattern and pushed a button. The remote switch had cut off the gas to the aircraft's engine. Even an expert pilot could not have guided the plane down to a safe spot in those mountains. There were no safe spots. The plane had crashed in a remote area north of Atlanta and that was it.

"How far have you taken this line of investigation?" I asked.

He didn't answer right away. Instead he got up and walked to the kitchen, rang a tiny silver bell and Juan reappeared as if by magic.

He said something to Juan in a low voice and Juan disappeared again. This guy was starting to give me the creeps. He was like a ninja, fading into the furniture.

"Juan will bring you a folder on my investigation regarding the airplane crash. You can take it with you. It contains everything that I have learned up to this point. If there are further lines of questioning, I will pay you. I've done my homework. Your firm will be paid a thousand dollars a day plus your personal expenses for travel, food and lodging. In addition I will give you another fifty thousand dollars if you find the person or persons who caused the death of my son-in-law and daughter, and fifty thousand more if you find Mona's killer."

"That isn't necessary," I said. "I want to do this for Tami."

"That is another matter," he said. "Tami is off limits to you, Kip. Whatever interest you have in Tami from this point forward will be strictly a matter of business. Is that understood?"

He handed me the folder.

He was crossing a line that I felt was none of his business, but for now I was willing to back off.

"Perfectly," I said.

CHAPTER TWENTY ONE

I took the folder directly to the library. It had become a temporary office for me. I had access to computers, it was quiet, and I had reference books for almost any subject. The digital age may someday replace printed books, but my personal feeling is that we will always need libraries.

I sat down in an area that had plush furniture, a small table next to a very comfortable chair. I spread the folder in my lap and started reading. Twenty minutes later I knew a lot more about airplanes than I did when I sat down. The folder had just about everything in it that a student pilot might have in his training folder. There were pages on proper flight plan filing, microphone procedures, altitudes, ground proximity devices, radar, glide slopes, bad weather procedures, instrument flying and a lot of things that were probably not going to do me any good.

I came across a piece of paper that appeared to be an inventory of sorts, and on closer examination found that it was a bill of materials for a Cessna 152, the type of plane that Harold Fawn had flown the day of the accident.

I put the paper on the bottom of the stack in the folder and picked up the next one. It was a black and white photograph. It showed a cylindrical shaped object, pretty badly burned. No identification was visible on it. Someone had written a note across the bottom of the picture with a permanent marker pen. "Fuel shut off, radio controlled".

That killed my idea about seeking the manufacturer and trying to find out who sold them, maybe with luck, who purchased this one. Then it occurred to me that if I had the actual object I might be able to clean it up and find a part number or manufacturer's name on it somewhere.

I shuffled through the documents and found a page near the bottom. It was a copy of a receipt for storage. The address was in Atlanta. Description of items stored "aircraft parts". The rental space was one similar to where I had secured the Austin Healey in Tallahassee, but slightly larger. This one was 10 by 12. The rent was $65 per month. The receipt was for storage from June, 1979 through November, 1979. At the top of the page was "Rented to" with the name of the renter blacked out. In the upper right hand corner was the number A3933. I didn't know what that number represented but I filed it away in the old memory bank.

The last piece of paper in the folder was a bill or invoice for services from a Miami Private Detective, Stan Morgan. His total bill, including expenses, was $11,290. I shuffled all of the papers and closed the folder on them and returned to the Lincoln. I dialed the number of the Miami PI on my cell phone and waited.

"Morgan Investigations," a pleasant female voice .

"Is Stan Morgan in?"

"One moment," she said.

I waited.

"Stan Morgan speaking," a man answered.

"Mr. Morgan, I'm a PI from Los Angeles, working a case here in the Miami area. I have a copy of an invoice you made regarding finding information about an aircraft accident north of Atlanta. The incident occurred in 1979, your invoice is dated a few years ago. Do you remember that case?"

"Yeah, I do," he said.

"I've been asked to look into it further." I said.

"By who?"

"Charles DuPont." I said.

"Wasn't he satisfied with my report?" he asked.

That confirmed something I had wondered about, who hired Morgan. Morgan was DuPont's information source.

"You'd have to ask him that," I said. "I'd just like to ask a few questions if you don't mind. I'll pay you for your time."

"Ask."

"I'd rather stop by your office and go over some things," I said.

"I charge $500 a day," he told me. "That's for an 8 hour day, how much time will this take?"

"Not more than an hour," I said. "I'll pay you $100 for an hour of your time, if I go over, I'll pay you another $100."

"10844 Adelaide St." he said. "Be here in an hour."

The line went dead. I keyed the address into the Lincoln's GPS system and left.

CHAPTER TWENTY TWO

Adelaide Street was one of those streets that can be found in almost any town in America. There were residential houses mixed with small strip malls, then more residential houses and more strip malls. Morgan's office at 10844 Adelaide was in an old residential dwelling that sat twenty feet from the sidewalk. It was a typical south Florida home, concrete block. It had not been stucco covered, however, just the raw blocks that looked out of place, like a Chevrolet parked in a Cadillac neighborhood.

I left the Lincoln at the curb and walked the 20 feet to the front door. I tried the knob and the door was locked. I rapped twice with my fist and waited.

Stan Morgan was about my size, much older than me but stocky and muscular. I took him to be in his early 70's. His graying hair stuck out from under a Fedora type hat that was also gray. He had on a black and white checked sports coat over a white shirt, no tie.

"You must be Yardley," he said when he opened the door. "Sorry about the locked door, but in this neighborhood you can't be too careful."

I looked around. The neighborhood didn't look all that bad to me, not like an East Los Angeles neighborhood, or one in the Watts area of LA.

"Come in," he said.

I went in and he closed the door behind me.

"You wanted to know about the accident case," he said, motioning me to sit down in a wooden chair that faced an old wooden desk. He walked behind the desk and sat in a wooden swivel chair that appeared about ready to collapse.

"What I'm really looking for is where that pile of aircraft metal might be stored today, if it is still stored somewhere."

"I doubt if that is true," he said. "That metal would have been sold for scrap by now. The rental was closed shortly after I took those pictures."

"You took these pictures?" I asked, and handed him the group of pictures from the folder I held in my hands.

He glanced through them.

156

"Yep."

"Weren't you curious about the radio controlled fuel shut off valve?"

"Curious in what way?"

"Like where it was made, who made it, a part number?"

"I thought of all of that," he said. "The problem was that it was burned so badly none of that information was readily available."

"Readily?"

"Well, it would have taken some time and money to figure out who made it. I wasn't sure that the guy that hired me would pay for me to go into further detail, so I never followed up on it."

"Charles DuPont paid you for the work?"

"Yeah. How is he? Still kicking?"

"I just talked to him this morning," I said. "He provided me with this folder, I'm guessing it was all work done by you regarding the investigation.'

"You guessed right," he said. "As far as I know I'm the only one who worked that case."

"So you didn't mention the radio controlled fuel shut off valve in your report?"

"Didn't think it was important," he said, glancing away.

Something didn't sound right to me. Morgan was being paid to investigate and he found the radio controlled fuel shut off valve but made no attempt to follow up on it. Either he intended to bargain for that information or someone else had got to him.

"Did you take this picture?" I showed him the picture of the fuel shut off valve.

"No," he said. That's not one of mine. I identify every copy that I take with an embossing stamp, like this one." He showed me an embossed set of initials, "SMI" on one of the other photos.

"Sam Morgan Investigations," he told me, pointing to the mark.

"Out of curiosity, do you know who rented the storage space where you found that stuff?"

"At the time I took those pictures the space was rented by the FAA. They had rental places all around the Atlanta airport with parts from different wrecks. Atlanta is the home of the Air Safety Board that investigates aircraft accidents."

"How long do they normally store that material?"

"Usually until they make a ruling as to the cause of the accident."

"They ruled the accident as bad weather and pilot error, didn't they? I think that was what I read in the newspaper files in the library."

"I wouldn't know about that," he said. "I didn't pay any attention to that at all."

"So you have no idea who took this picture of the fuel shut off valve?"

"Nope," he said. "I remember seeing that thing when I took the other pictures. It didn't look like it belonged to the rest of the wreckage, so I ignored it. The FAA guy I talked to didn't think it was important either."

"Well, I think that's all the questions I have," I said. I pulled out my wallet and extracted a $100 bill. "This should cover your time. Thanks for co-operating."

Stan Morgan's eyes lit up and the sight of the bill, he took it rather quickly from my hand and smiled.

"Any time, Yardley," he said. "If you need a consultant on this case, let me know. I'm available."

I made a mental note to do a check on Stan Morgan's finances, shook his hand and left.

CHAPTER TWENTY THREE

I drove back to the library. Before going in, I got the folder out and looked for the name of the rental place, Acme rentals, and used my cell phone to dial the number shown at the top of the page.

I was amazed when someone answered. It had crossed my mind that the price of real estate had gone up so much that the rentals may have been torn down and replaced by office buildings or homes.

"I'm looking for information regarding an invoice from 1979. I don't suppose you could tell me who rented the space, if I gave you the number?"

"What is the number?" a voice asked.

"A3933." I said.

Silence. I was beginning to think I'd lost my connection when the person came back on line.

"Yes, Sir," the voice said. "That space was rented to store material from an aircraft accident. The Air Safety Board was the renter."

"Do you have a name? Perhaps the name of the agent?"

"No sir, that information isn't on our copy. Oh, wait a minute, my computer shows that the space was rented twice. Let me check the next record. Oh, here it is, the second time it was rented was by a man named DuPont."

"DuPont?" I asked.

"Yes, Sir. A ValJean DuPont."

"DuPont was an agent for the Air Safety Board?"

"I wouldn't know about that, Sir," the voice said. "It has his signature as renter."

I thought about that for a long moment. The voice thought I had disconnected.

"Was there something else?"

"Can you tell me, by chance, what happened to the material that was being stored? Was it sold for scrap?"

"One moment."

I waited. After a few minutes the voice returned.

"Something strange," the voice said. "Our records show that another space was rented next to A3933. A3935 records has a note. 'material from A3933' written across the bottom."

"What about that space? Do you have records of what happened to that one?"

"It's still rented." the voice said.

"What?"

"It's still being rented," the voice told me. "Has been paid monthly since 1979 by the same account."

"Do you have a name?"

"Same name. ValJean DuPont."

"Thank you." I said. "You've been a help."

That information sank like a ticking time bomb in the gray matter of my brain. What did ValJean DuPont have to do with the Air Safety Board? Or, for that matter, what did he have to do with the accident that took the lives of Harold and Harriet Fawn?

It was time for me to pay ValJean another visit.

I needed more information, however, and took my folder into the library.

I sat in the same spot that I had used previously, connected to the internet on the computer and started researching ValJean DuPont.

Aside from vital statistics, date of birth and so forth, I was particularly interested in ValJean's employment record.

I found an article in the local newspaper that intrigued me. ValJean DuPont was promoted to Senior Programming Manager at Commodity Computer Systems, Miami. I looked up Commodity Computer Systems and discovered that it was the computer programming firm that had been started by Harold Fawn, and sold after his death. The new owner was William Stevens.

Where had I heard that name?

I glanced back through my note book. I'm a meticulous note taker. I carry a notebook with me even when I'm not working a case, but particularly when I'm investigating.

The notebook I had now was encased in mock leather, and had been given to me by Rhonda.

I flipped through the pages looking for the name. William Stevens. There it was. He was the Chairman of the Miami/Dade County school board, and a real estate developer. I remembered trying to contact him a few days earlier, but it had been on a Saturday. I thought it was time to pay a visit to Mr. Stevens. Right after I got some answers from ValJean DuPont.

CHAPTER TWENTY FOUR

A half hour later I stood next to the spot where I had last talked to ValJean DuPont. ValJean's geodesic raft boat was gone. He had borrowed some money from me, ostensibly to get some wire to fix a faulty air conditioner. I know he was hurting for a drink when he drove away.

Now I knew nothing.

I walked back to the Lincoln and drove the short distance to the Harbor Master's office, got out and went inside.

"Any idea where Val Jan DuPont took his raft?"

I motioned out the open door towards the end of the pier where ValJean's raft had been the last time I saw it.

A young man looked surprised and jumped up quickly from his chair. I think I caught him playing computer games on his desktop computer.

"Is he gone?"

"Well his raft is gone," I said. "Unless someone other than ValJean took it, I'm assuming he is gone too."

The uniformed young man stepped by me and to the door. He stepped outside onto the pier decking and looked in the direction where ValJean's raft had been.

"I'll be damned," was all he said.

"I'm guessing he didn't tell you when he left?"

"Why no. He normally will tell me if he's going out in the bay on a fishing trip, or up the coast a ways. Sometimes he takes that contraption of a boat up the coast to some kind of meeting place where a bunch of folks with like minds gather to discuss the advantages of building geodesic homes. Matter of fact, they're meeting there this month."

"Where would that be?" I asked.

"Up at Palmetto Bay," he said. "Not more than an hour drive from here."

"How will I know when I'm there?" I asked.

"When you head east, off of highway one, there'll be a souvenir shop on your right. Stop there and ask where the geodesic dome people are meeting. They'll know."

I thanked him and left.

An hour later I made the turn off of the highway and headed East towards Palmetto Bay. I saw Conch's Souvenirs on my right and pulled into a sandy parking lot. The place was packed with tourists. I found a parking place near the far end of the lot and locked the Lincoln.

It was nearing two in the afternoon and the sun was hot. I was thankful for the air-conditioning inside the building. People swarmed around all of the tables looking at tee shirts, conch shells, baubles, bangles and beads. It was a typical souvenir shop. The front counter, near the door, was manned by a dumpy woman wearing a muumuu and about fifteen pounds of makeup. A skinny tourist man was buying a straw hat and some shells. I sidled in behind him and waited.

When he had his change he stepped aside and started stuffing bills back in his wallet. The dumpy woman grinned at me and asked if she could help me. When she saw that I was empty handed, her grin changed to a frown.

"I just wanted to know if you could tell me where the geodesic dome people are meeting?"

"Those crazies?" she asked. "Go on out this road towards the pier. When you get to the end, it will turn right and left. Take the left turn and go about a quarter of a mile. There's a park on the left and that's where them idiots are talking. Them danged geodesics won't stand up to a hurricane, I don't know why they bother building 'em."

"Thank you, lovely lady," I said. Her grin returned just as fast as it had faded. I laid five dollars on the table and asked for a Florida key chain that hung on a rack next to the cash register. I didn't particular want the key chain, but I wanted her to remember me.

I found the park without difficulty. As I walked through it, after parking the Lincoln, I was looking seaward to see if I could catch a glimpse of the geodesic raft that ValJean DuPont might have brought. I saw a lot of boats but nothing resembling the raft.

I found a stage with a speaker making his pitch for his product, a foldable geodesic tent. I listened a minute then walked to a table next to the stage. There it appeared that people were paying for their turn to pitch their product. A man sat near a small green metal box, counting money. Other speakers were waiting nearby for their opportunity to speak. I asked if ValJean DuPont had registered.

"Not yet," I was told. "I'm not sure he's coming this year," the man said. "He was here last year and spoke for a half an hour about his plans for building the safest geodesic raft available. He had solar panels, wiring diagrams, instruction kits and the whole nine yards of wax to sell."

I wondered what he meant by nine yards of wax but decided he had mixed his metaphors a little and thought nothing of it.

"So you haven't seen him this year?" I asked.

"No, Sir," he said. "If I see him, can I give him a message?"

I gave him one of my cards with my cell phone number on it and told him that I would appreciate it if ValJean showed up, to have him call me.

"Will do!" he said, smiling. "Are you a dome enthusiast?"

"I'm interested," I said. "But I need to talk to ValJean first."

That seemed to satisfy him. I walked away, towards the pier area, my eyes still searching for the half a dome I expected to see sitting in the marina somewhere. I saw nothing. I retreated to the Lincoln and got in and closed the door and relaxed in the cooler interior, wondering what my next move should be.

On a hunch I dialed Happs' number. When he came on the line I told him that I was looking for ValJean DuPont and asked if he had any idea where the eccentric rafter might be.

"Hard to say," Happs said. "I've known him to go all the way up the coast as far as the Jacksonville area, but then he may have gone south, too. He has spent some time in the Everglades, fishing. Since he lost his leg and went on disability he has fished a lot. There's no telling where he went."

"O.K." I said. "Thanks, Happs. I'll look for him."

"Let me know if you find him, OK? If I don't hear from you in three days I'll ask my people to keep an eye out for him."

"I'll do that, and thanks," I said.

Just as I hung up I heard the sound of a horn and glanced around to see who had honked. There was a blue pick-up truck parked next to me. An older man waved and then got out of the truck and approached the

Lincoln. I hit the button and rolled the window down.

"You looking for ValJean?" he asked.

"Yes, have you seen him?"

"No, but I was supposed to meet with him here to discuss building more geodesic rafts. I live in Coral Gables and have a small manufacturing plant. We thought we could build the geodesic rafts and sell them locally."

"Is there that much of a market?" I asked him.

"From what ValJean tells me, there's enough interest to manufacture a hundred a year. That's quite enough, I'd think. Are you interested in building dome rafts?"

"No, my interest in ValJean right at this moment has nothing to do with rafts. I'm a private investigator from Los Angeles." I showed him my ID. "I just need to ask ValJean some questions about an airplane accident a few years ago."

"Airplane accident? That's a coincidence. ValJean did some work on my airplane for me. I've got a Piper Cub. It's an old one, but I love it. Do you fly?"

"No, Sir," I said. "My wings aren't feathered enough."

He laughed.

"If I could fly, I'd search the coast line for ValJean's raft boat."

"I can do that," he said. "Would you like to go looking for him with me, in my Piper Cub?"

"You don't mind doing that?" I asked.

"I wouldn't mind doing it. ValJean and I have become pretty good friends."

He stuck out his hand. "I'm Spencer Adams."

"Kip Yardley," I said, shaking his hand. His grip was firm and his arms were muscular. I guessed his age at about seventy.

"My plane is at Coral Gables airport, Kip." he said. "If you'd like to follow me, we can be there in a half an hour. It's all fueled and ready to fly. We've got three or four hours before sunset, we can fly all the way to the tip of Key West in that length of time and be back before dark."

"Sounds good to me, Spencer," I said.

"Please call me Spence," he said, "That's what the guys back home called me."

"Where's home?" I asked.

"Green Village, Tennessee," he said. "I was sheriff there for 20 years. I retired five years ago and came down here to play golf. I started doing some tinkering with a golf cart and came up with an idea that has taken off good. I manufacture plastic domes to replace the tops on standard golf carts, sell them to cart owners up north where the weather is a little colder in winter."

"Sounds like a good idea," I said. "How do you get in and out of a cart like that?"

"They're made in two parts," he said. "The front half slides back into the back half, and in good weather you can just leave the front part back. In cold weather or rain, you slide it forward and you are in a bubble. Small fans keep fresh air coming in. I also designed a heater that runs off of the exhaust system. Sales have been good. I'm a very fortunate man."

"I'll follow you, Sheriff," I said.

"Please, don't call me sheriff. Spence or Spencer, but I had enough of sheriff to last me a lifetime."

"OK, Spence," I said. "Lead on. I'm anxious to take that flight. Maybe later you and I can play some golf."

"Now you're talking," he grinned and got in his truck.

CHAPTER TWENTY FIVE

The view from 1500 feet up in the air was fantastic. Afternoon sun lit up the entire shoreline of Florida. The winds were quiet and the little two seater purred like a kitten, or a Cub, appropriately. The aircraft was a PA15 Vagabond, I sat side by side with Spence in the two seat aircraft, and watched the area below the right side of the aircraft. Spence was watching out of the left side. We stayed at 1500 feet, out of the glide path for commercial aircraft and flew south along the coast line.

ValJean's raft boat had a big red X painted on top of it and it would be readily visible, although it would look like a tea cup from this height. The sun glistened off of the still waters of Biscayne Bay as if the water was a billion pieces of broken glass. Further inland, the land mass resembled a checkerboard, agriculture areas with a million little lakes interspersed between them. Highways, like shoe laces, stretched north and south with little play cars traversing them.

We flew the coast line all the way to Flamingo, then followed the Buttonwood Canal north to Coot Bay, where Spence said that ValJean liked to fish. We saw nothing that resembled the strange geodesic dome raft boat.

"He might have went further west and came back into the Everglades from the west," Spence said. "Do you want to fly that way?"

"Are we safe on fuel and time?" I asked.

"We've got enough fuel," he told me. "I think we will be cutting it pretty close to get back before dark. I can land after dark but I don't like to, my eyes aren't what they used to be."

"Let's head back then," I said. "I thank you for your time, and I'll send you a check for fuel."

He turned the small aircraft to the east and we were flying away from the sun. As the aircraft banked I caught a glimpse of something bright near the eastern limit of Coots Bay, reflecting the sun. It looked like a mirror. I looked again and it was gone. Could have been the sun reflecting off the windshield of a boat, I thought.

We flew back without talking much, I asked Spence if he knew what ValJean DuPont did for a living before he lost his leg. He told me that he thought ValJean was a mechanic, since that's all he had ever known him to do. I asked if ValJean ever mentioned computers and Spence said that he knew ValJean was smart about them, but didn't know he had ever worked with them.

"At one point in his life he was a programmer for a company called Commodity Computer Systems," I said. "They were once owned by Harold Fawn, and taken over by William Spencer after Fawn was killed in an airplane crash back in 1979."

"That's the crash you are investigating?" he asked.

"Yes," I said.

"Good luck," he replied. "It's hard to come up with anything thirty years after it happens."

We continued to chat amicably as we flew back to Coral Gables. Spence landed the Piper Cub with ease and taxied into a hangar. I thanked him again and gave him one of my cards along with a promise to send him a check.

"Forget the fuel," he said. "I needed some flight time and I enjoyed it. It's nice to meet you, Kip Yardley, and I hope to see you again sometime. If you ever change your mind about building a geodesic dome boat, look me up. And if you need a dome top for your golf cart, I'm on the internet."

We shook hands and I walked to the parking lot and got in the Lincoln. It had been a long day and I wanted to get back to Tami, even though her great grandfather had seemed adamant about my relationship with her.

CHAPTER TWENTY SIX

After a quiet, uneventful, evening with Tami, where we talked about things other than Mona's death, the lotto ticket, and my investigation, I drove back to my motel room, swam in the pool for an hour, then went to bed. My mind must have kept right on working after I fell asleep, I awoke at 5 a.m. with the distinct feeling that I was missing something.

Most of us have felt that feeling at some point in our lives. It was like I was forgetting something, something I was supposed to do, or something I was supposed to read, or a bill I was supposed to pay. I couldn't quite get my mind to settle on the issue, but the feeling was persistent. Something was there, my mind was trying to make it come to the surface, but self doubt, like the shallow waters of the Everglades, kept pushing it down. Down into the muck on the bottom.

By the time I had eaten breakfast in the hotel café and pondered on what course of action I was going to take, the thought started rising to the surface. It was slow, but after I showered, shaved and got dressed for the day, it was clearer.

Stan Morgan had lied to me.

He knew the significance of the fuel shut off valve and had purposefully withheld that knowledge from Charles DuPont.

He said that it wasn't his photograph. He had even shown me his mark on the rest of the papers. I took the folder out and sat on the edge of the bed in my room and spread the papers out on the bed.

The copy of the photograph appeared out of place immediately. All of the rest of the pages were eight and a half by eleven. That page had been cropped. Not electronically, but physically. It was eight and a half wide, but an inch had been cut off of the bottom.

Somehow Charles DuPont had acquired the Xeroxed photograph, but I was thinking that it was not part of the package provided by Morgan. Someone else had discovered the photograph and given it to DuPont.

Morgan had seemed a little skittish when I visited him. His door had been locked and he appeared as if he was being cautious about who he talked to. His reason for talking to me was motivated by money. It finally dawned on me that Morgan had been working two sides of the case when he worked for Charles DuPont. Someone was paying him to give DuPont only the answers that the unknown someone wanted him to have.

That made me more curious about the fuel shut off valve picture. I decided to send the copy of the picture to a friend of mine back in LA who had come through for me several times in past cases.

Richard Rheames is a bachelor friend that I had lived next to in Long Beach when I started doing PI work. We had shared some Saturday afternoon pool parties, barbecues, and baseball games. He was still a student at UCLA, even though he was approaching middle age. He loved the single life and had no constant female companions, although some of the dames he dated were classy, good looking ladies.

He was employed in a research lab at UCLA and had acquired his masters degree in chemical analysis, now he was studying for a doctorate. I decided that I would send him the picture of the fuel cell and see if he could get any leads on it. Without the real item, I thought that his help would be stymied, but then he had pulled some rabbits out of the bag for me in the past, so I would try again.

I could have faxed a copy to Richard, but for some reason I had left Richard's phone and fax number out of the new notebook that Rhonda had given me. I drove to an Office Depot and purchased an envelope, addressed it carefully from memory, and put the picture in it, along with a note asking Richard to see if he could identify the valve. I inquired about a post office and the clerk told me that there was one in the mall across the street. I decided to walk, the day was beautiful and I had not been getting a lot of exercise, other than swimming.

Half way across the parking lot I saw three men approaching, one from my right, one from the left and one coming straight at me. They were not cops, I could tell that at a glance. The clothes they wore were too expensive and flashy for cops.

I kept walking straight, and the two men on either side of me fell in behind me and in an instant they grabbed my arms, one pulled one way and the other pulled the opposite way. Old age has its advantage. At a point where your body starts to slow down, your brain tries to make up the difference. It was the old adage, 'work smarter, not harder' that ran through my mind. The man approaching facing me stopped five feet in front of me, too far away for a front kick.

"This is your final warning, dumb shit," the man facing me said. "You mess with Al again and you die."

He took a step towards me, drew back his fist, all the way back, for a long swing. I could see a big ring on he third finger of his right hand. It had two letters shaped with diamonds. G.G.

The message my brain had sent me to work smarter, not harder, caused me to react immediately with one of the oldest tricks in self defense. I leaned hard to my left and at the same time pulled hard with my right hand. Using the force of the man who was already pulling on my left arm, the combined force pulled the man on my right towards me. I raised my right leg and side kicked him in the groin. He released his hold on my arm.

The unexpected release of the force on my right, let me go freely to the left, along with the pull of the man on my left. I whirled on my left foot, planted my right foot firmly, dropped my right shoulder and lashed out with a wicked knife hand thrust and caught the attacker in the throat. I heard him gurgle but wasn't watching his reaction. The man who had been facing me had launched his swing, missing my midsection. My body was now facing ninety degrees to the left and his body was perpendicular to mine, on my right.

The guy on my left had dropped my arm and grabbed his throat. With both hands free, I knew I had a chance against the goon who had tried to slug me in the gut.

I dropped to the pavement on my right palm and spun my body, hard and quick to my right, left leg extended, sweeping my left foot out. It caught the guy behind his knees and he fell face forward.

Several people had started yelling. An old woman had let out a scream, and a crowd had started to collect around us.

As the thug fell I brought my right arm back fast, fist clenched, and clipped him in the back of his neck with my elbow. He continued his forward fall and his nose and forehead hit the pavement with a solid thunk.

I glanced to my right and saw the right hand of that bozo start up. It held a gun. I ducked to a squatting position as the gun fired. I could feel the heat from the discharge but the slug went wild over my head. Somebody else screamed. I dove straight at the gunner's midsection, ramming my head into his gut as hard as I could. He fell backwards. His butt hit the concrete as I regained my balance and stood up. His right hand with the gun was arcing back towards me just as I kicked his head, under his chin. Blood spurted from his mouth.

I saw my chance and kept moving in the direction of the kick, stepped through the gathering circle of people and ran like hell.

"Call the police," I yelled and kept right on moving.

I ran through the door of the mall and glanced around. I was in the food court. To my right I saw a sign. "Restrooms". There was a long corridor. Down the way I could see several women waiting in line to use the restroom, but fortunately the line for the men's room was short, a middle aged man and a man in his late twenties with a little boy.

"Excuse me," I said and slipped ahead of them into the men's room. I locked myself in a stall and dropped the lid on the commode. I sat down, breathing hard. My pulse was racing and I could feel my heart beating in my chest. I realized that soon I was going to have to do one of two things, carry a big gun or give up being a private detective.

But for now I wasn't ready to do the latter, so it looked like I was going to have to do the former.

I sat on the commode until my heart quit racing. I couldn't hear any commotion so I opened the stall door a little, peaked out and didn't see any of the three men who had attacked me. One or two of them might not be in condition to create further danger, but I wasn't sure. The man with the young kid gave me a dirty look but moved aside when I sneered at him.

I exited the restroom and looked back towards the food court. Nothing. I could hear a siren in the background each time someone came through the main mall door. It would seem loud, then fade when the door shut, then loud again as the door opened.

I walked to a spot where I could see the mall door and waited. People were coming and going as if nothing had happened. Then a few started gathering at the door, now and then someone would make a motion like a man shooting a gun, finger extended, thumb up, then point to the parking lot. Everyone had their own tale to tell. I had a tale to tell Detective Lt. Happs the next time I saw him. I also had an envelope to mail and a message to send.

The envelope was to Richard Rheames. The message was to Alfredo Sarcosi.

CHAPTER TWENTY SEVEN

When I want to know something about someone I always rely on my source in California, Toby Smith. Toby and I had attended college together, joined the California Highway Patrol together, and were best of friends. He had helped me on many instances where vital information was part of the puzzle. Now I needed to know some things about Alfredo Sarcosi.

The admonition given me by Charles DuPont to not mess with the mob man was strong in my mind. My reply to him was stronger. Show no fear. But the truth of the matter was that I knew very little about Sarcosi other than his alleged ties to the mafia. I needed more. If I wanted to plan something to send a definite message to Alfredo Sarcosi, I needed to find out more about him. One thing I will never do is make a personal assault on someone's family to get even with the enemy. Unless the family is part and parcel of the enemy, as in the case of Alfredo Sarcosi, Jr.

I called Toby's office, and was surprised when a secretary put me through to him.

"Toby, Old Pal, Old Buddy," I said.

"Oh God," he moaned. "What do you want now? If it's money, you've got more than me, if it is pity, I feel sorry for you, if it is help, you're too far away, and too far gone."

"It's information," I said.

"Isn't it always?"

"Alfredo Sarcosi," I said. "Alleged minor member of the New York mob. Owns a deli in Miami. His son is Alfredo, Jr. Both are getting under my skin a little. Before I send him a 'back off' message, I need to know more about him."

"Spell that," he said.

"S-A-R-C-O-S-I. Alfredo, A-L...."

"I know how to spell Alfredo," he grunted.

"Think you can help me?" I asked.

"Maybe," he said. "I don't know anyone in Miami who can help, but I know lots of people in New York. If he's connected up there, I might be able to find something."

"Or if he's from New York?" I said, the thought suddenly crossing my mind.

"Right." Toby said. "Any idea how long he's been in the Miami area?"

"Since 1979," I said. "Thirty years?"

"Age?"

"Somewhere around sixty, I'd guess," I told him.

"Let me do some checking," Toby said. "I'll call you on your cell phone if I get anything. May take a couple of days, might be as early as this afternoon. What have you got against him?"

"His goons just tried to blow me away after they found they couldn't beat the crap out of me."

"Goons? More than one? You must still be in good shape, Old Buddy. Still practicing Karate?"

"Haven't been to class since I left LA," I said. "And I'm getting more out of shape every day I get older."

"If there were two, I'd say you are still in fighting shape. If there were more than two, I'd say you are still in excellent shape. How many goons were there?"

"Three," I said. "But only one got off a shot."

"Have you described them to the local authorities?"

"Not yet, Toby," I said. "I want to keep them out of it until I can't see any other way out. That's why I'm calling you."

"Is this a personal thing, or is this guy, Alfredo Sarcosi, involved in a case you are investigating? And what kind of case have you got yourself mixed up with in Florida?"

"Murder." I said. "And I'm not sure about the involvement. If I find out Sarcosi did it I'll let you know. Right after I hit him between the eyes with a nine iron."

"Played any golf?" he asked.

"Nope. I am going to play when I get to Kentucky, but that trip will have to wait awhile. Call me when you get something, Toby, please?"

"OK Kip," he said. "I don't have to tell you to be careful. Those kind of folks have resources that can get to you. If they can get the President of the United States, they can get anyone."

Toby believed, as I do, that the mob was part of the assassination of John Kennedy.

"OK Toby. I'll be careful. And thanks, pal."

"Bye," he said.

I had been standing just outside Victoria's Secrets in the mall as I talked to Toby, and didn't realize that as I talked I was looking at all the display dummies. Several women passed me giving me dirty looks like I was a pervert of some kind. I snapped the phone shut and waked on down the mall passageway towards a JC Penny's and a Sears store, my face turning a crimson shade of red.

I walked through Sears and found an exit on the opposite side of the mall from where I entered. I walked outside, then back to the Penny's entrance and went back in, glancing over my shoulder to make sure I wasn't being followed. I slipped through Penny's, to the mall interior, stopped and looked at the direction board and found the Post Office Annex. I mailed the package to Richard Rheames and left the mall to the senior citizens morning walkers and made my way back to the Lincoln, avoiding the police squad cars near the entrance to the food court.

CHAPTER TWENTY EIGHT

At eight o'clock the next morning, my new-found friend, Spencer Adams, dressed in his old Green Village, Tennessee Sheriff's uniform, walked into Sarcosi's Deli.

Toby had called me late on Friday evening and given me the rundown on Alfredo Sarcosi.

He had been kicked out of school in the 9th grade for stealing money from a teacher's desk. Prior to that he had been suspended several times for extorting kids lunch money, smoking, starting fights, and poor grades. His first visit to jail was for holding up a liquor store. When he told the clerk to put a bottle of Jack Daniels in the bag with the cash, she told him he wasn't old enough to drink and that she would need to see his ID.

He had shown her his driver's license to prove he was 21.

Not too smart. I wondered when he had obtained enough intelligence to run a deli, but when I checked out his license for the place I found that it was in his wife's name. She was the brains behind the business. Yet, from what Toby told me, Sarcosi might be a rising star in the Miami mob sky.

I was standing near the deli counter, dressed in blue jeans and a sweat shirt that had "Florida Gators" across the front. I had a false beard and mustache and dark glasses.

Spencer had a clipboard in his hand, a new fake badge pinned on his shirt, and was making his debut as an actor on my behalf. He asked for Sarcosi, and when the big hairy deli owner came out of his office, Spencer Adams handed him a fake document.

It stated that the Deli must be inspected for suspected violation of a code that did not exist in the Miami-Dade County Restaurant and Food Services book that Spencer Adams carried with him. A new page had been inserted in the book by me.

It stated if samples of the business establishment's water contained dihydrogen monoxide, they were in violation. The document read that Saracosi had to close for two days or until such time as they complied with the regulation. To comply, they had to test the water daily and if it turned litmus paper either red or blue, they must remain closed.

Spencer Adams carried a small vial of vinegar diluted with water until it was just acidic enough to turn a strip of blue litmus paper to red. He also carried litmus paper strips in his shirt pocket.

Spencer, with a great deal of authority in his voice, demanded a sample of the water.

Sarcosi got a glass and filled it with water from the tap. Spencer Adams, with enough aplomb to make the late Art Carney laugh, flourished the vial of diluted vinegar, dumped it in the glass of water, picked a swizzle stick from his pocket and stirred it. Then he dipped the end of a piece of litmus paper in the solution. It immediately turned red.

Sarcosi watched, with a puzzled, half frightened look on his face.

"Sorry, Sir," Adams said. "As you can plainly see, your water contains dihydrogen monoxide. You'll have to close. Take these strips and test it every day. When it doesn't turn the strips either red or blue, you can open again."

Sarcosi took the strips.

I was laughing under my breath so hard I damn near peed my pants.

A tiny giggle finally escaped, but I covered it by coughing loudly.

Sarcosi had a crestfallen look.

"How bad is that stuff?" Sarcosi asked.

"Well, read what it says here in the book," Spencer said, showing Sarcosi the page I had copied from the internet and inserted in the book.

"I don't have my glasses, can you read it for me?" Sarcosi said.

"Says here that it is called hydroxyl acid, a major component of acid rain. You've heard of acid rain, haven't you?"

"Yeah."

"It contributes to the greenhouse effect, may cause severe burns if heated to 212 degrees Farenheit, fatal if inhaled, contributes to the erosion of land, accelerates corrosion and rusting of metal, cause of many electrical failures and decreases the ability of automobile brakes to function properly in wet weather."

"Wow," Sarcosi said.

"Yeah," Spencer Adams said. "Also, it is used as an industrial solvent and coolant. A major component of nuclear power plants, as a fire retardant, and in the production of Styrofoam."

"All of that, huh?"

"Yep. Some bad stuff," Adams said, stifling a grin that I could see from ten feet away.

"How long will it take for the city to fix my water?" He asked.

"That's hard to say, Sir," Adams quipped. "It may be a week or even two weeks. Even after items are washed, this stuff is still contaminating them. I'll come back in a week and test it again. Now if you'll just sign this to show that I have been here and tested your water, I'll be on my way. Thanks for your cooperation."

Sarcosi took the clip board and pen and signed the paper.

"Yeah," he mumbled. "Your welcome, I guess."

I dang near choked.

We sat in Spencer Adams' truck laughing as we watched Sarcosi flip the sign on his front door from "Open" to "Closed" then the lights went off inside the Deli. Sarcosi appeared at the door, opened it and walked out, ushering the Cuban helper in front of him, then turned and locked the door. Spencer Adams was beating on his steering wheel, laughing loud enough to be heard back in Coral Gables if the truck windows had not been up and the air conditioner running.

Pay backs are hell.

CHAPTER TWENTY NINE

Monday morning. I paid a visit to William Stevens. He was a big man, at least four inches taller than I, and somewhere around two hundred and fifty pounds. His hands were very big, nails trimmed to perfection, a golden ring on he 3rd finger of his left hand. He wore a light gray silk suit and long sleeved shirt with French cuffs.

He had a head of pure white hair, a little thin, with elements of a pink scalp showing through. His smile appeared as though it had been surgically implanted. One of those phony, politician type smiles that I have grown to hate.

His secretary had disappeared behind a walnut paneled door, closed the door behind her, and then reappeared a full minute later, holding the door open.

"Mr. Stevens will see you now, Mr. Yardley."

That always made me wonder if the guy was blind and suddenly regained his vision. It's a miracle!!

I stood in front of his desk and thought about what I wanted to ask him. I hadn't really made any notes or planned the visit, it was going to be a shot in the dark.

"Have a seat, Mr. Yardley," he said, in a voice so deep that I instinctively backed up a step to keep from falling in the well that it came from.

I sat down in a plush chair with shiny wooden arms.

"My secretary tells me you wanted to see me about ValJean DuPont?"

"I am a private investigator, Mr. Stevens," I said, as a beginner. "I've been hired by Charles DuPont to investigate the murder of his granddaughter, Mona. In my investigation I ran across some things that I need to speak to ValJean DuPont about. When I drove to his space at the marina, his boat was gone."

"That isn't surprising," he said. "ValJean is a bit eccentric. He's been known to take that contraption of a boat all the way to Georgia. Did you think I would know his whereabouts, Yardley?"

"Actually I wanted to ask you about his employment with Commodity Computer

Systems. I understand that you are the owner of that company?"

"Yes, that is one of my holdings," he said. "I have invested in several small companies."

He didn't offer any details, so I asked.

"Is real estate your major investment portfolio?"

"Developing real estate," he said. "I own a construction company that buys property and develops it. I am on the board of three banks here in Miami, and I am the Superintendent of the Miami-Dade county school system, among other things."

"But you didn't come here to ask questions about me, did you? What is it you want to know, exactly, Mr. Yardley?"

"What position ValJean DuPont had with Commodity Computer Systems before he lost his leg and retired." I said.

"He was a senior programmer. His primary responsibility was to monitor the software used by the Florida Lotto Commission to track their sales, their profits and the reporting of winnings to the press."

"Did ValJean develop that software?"

"No, I don't think he was that astute, Mr. Yardley," Stevens said. "Although he was a brilliant employee, at least that is what I am told, I think his ability was more in the field of maintaining the software, working out the glitches, implementing new additions as the needs arose."

"Can you tell me just what it is that the software does? What function it has in the actual drawing of the numbers?"

"I'm not sure I know what you mean, Yardley," he said.

"Well, I know that within hours of the actual drawing, the lotto people can tell where the winning number was sold, the date it was sold, and how many different tickets were sold with all or part of the winning numbers. Does the software you say ValJean DuPont was maintaining run that function?"

"Yes, that would all be driven by the main body of the software that ValJean administered." he said.

"Can you tell me anything about how the money is divided if there are no winners?"

"Each time there is a drawing, if there are no winners, a certain percentage of the income goes towards the administration of the program, that is each vendor that sells lotto tickets gets paid for selling them, a percentage goes to the State of Florida for their general fund, and of course the major portion rolls over as the prize for the next drawing."

"And are those figures all compiled based on the software program that ValJean DuPont administered?"

"Yes," he said, rubbing a huge hand through his thick mop of white hair. "He was in charge of that general administration of the software package."

"When did he leave the company?" I asked.

"Fifteen years ago was when he lost his leg. He left the company after that, taking his pension early and of course his invested funds as well."

"How did he lose his leg?"

"Well, I can tell you it wasn't in the war," he said. "ValJean served in the Armed Forces, however that rumor about him losing his leg in combat is just that, a rumor. I've heard the tale about the alligator, and I'm not sure I believe that one."

"Did ValJean have a substance abuse problem while employed by your company?" I asked.

"If he did I knew nothing about it," he said. "The company is actually ran by someone I hired who has significant expertise. I'm sure that the President of the company would not have tolerated a known substance abuse problem."

"How about after he left the company?" I asked.

"That would be none of my concern, Mr. Yardley. I knew ValJean as an employee of one of my companies, but I know nothing of his personal life, nor do I care to. The information regarding his boat is all something I gleaned from local news broadcast. He's become quite a character in the Everglades, and local television stations have covered some of his exploits."

I was silent for a few seconds. Too many seconds, I guess, for William Stevens.

"Was there something else, Mr. Yardley?"

"Not right now," I said. "If I think of something, may I call you?"

"If it is in regards to ValJean DuPont, I'm afraid I don't have anything further. If it concerns Commodity Computer Systems, I'd prefer you call Mr. Patrick Checkers, the president and general manager."

"Of course," I said. What I was thinking was that I needed to find out more about the way the school system handled money that was given to them from the Lotto Commission. That would have to wait, I surmised.

CHAPTER THIRTY

The offices of Miami's prominent psychologist, Doctor Roflecion, were located a block away from the police station. I made it a point to call Tami and tell her that I intended to talk to the good doctor to see if I could determine why Mona could not read at an adult level.

I didn't have any idea why I thought that was important to the case, but the thought kept nagging me like a stiff label in a shirt, rubbing the back of my neck and not letting me put it aside. The only relief is to take the shirt off. That's why I stepped inside the cool building and asked a pretty receptionist if I could see Doctor Roflecion. The name would have been perfect for a psychologist if it had been spelled with an "e" as the second letter, instead of the "o". REFLEXION. Reflexes...my thoughts were scattered as I waited in the reception area.

"Doctor Roflecion will see you now," I heard, through the jumbled thoughts.

"Thank you," I said, and rose and walked through the door to an inner office.

There wasn't a desk in the office, just a small table with a few books on it, a leather bound writing tablet, and a pencil. Aside from a filing cabinet, a "living room" atmosphere prevailed, with soft leather couch and recliner. Doctor Roflecion sat on the couch.

She smiled at me but didn't get up, just crossed her long, beautiful legs, and extended her hand.

"I have a few minutes before my next appointment, Mr. Yardley," she said. "What is it you wish to speak to me about?"

I had not expected a female psychologist, and stammered a little before getting my question clear in my own mind.

"Without compromising patient/doctor confidentiality, can you tell me your diagnosis regarding Mona Fawn's regression of reading abilities?"

"First, Mr. Yardley, please tell me what your interest is in Mona's problem," she said.

"Oh, I'm sorry," I stammered. "You must have heard about Mona's death. I've been retained by her grandfather, Charles DuPont, to try to solve the mystery of her death, and the death of her parents in a tragic plane wreck."

"Well you have pretty much answered your own question, Mr. Yardley," she said, smiling and showing sparkling white teeth. She was a very beautiful woman, and I was thinking that she knew how to use her beauty.

"Sometimes tragic, and unexpected events, can trigger something in a person's mind that will make them try to blank out the event. In Mona's case, it may have been something that she read about the accident that caused that trigger. It's hard to say exactly what triggered her regression, but I do know that she was an honor student prior to the accident. And tests showed that even though her reading regression continued in her adult life, she was within the top 10 percent of the general population as far as her intelligence quotient is concerned. She had an IQ of 137 on the Stanford-Binet scale."

"So what you are telling me is that you have no idea what caused her regression?"

"I have a lot of "ideas" but nothing that can pinpoint it to an absolute," she said. "Psychology is all about so called "ideas" Mr. Yardley. It is not an absolute science, and that is a good thing. Everyone's mind behaves in a different pattern based on their own brain waves, physical and mental health, and many other factors, including environment and heredity. Nothing is cast in steel when it relates to psychology. Oh sure, there are some guidelines that we use, but I'll be the first to admit that we really do not know what makes people tick."

She had expressed my feelings about psychology to the "T" and I told her so.

"That makes you a unique individual, Mr. Yardley," she said. "Most of the general population believe that we can work miracles. We don't have all the answers, just the proper questions. We ask the right questions and our patients cure themselves by revealing their innermost thoughts. Once we have the answers that the patients provide, we can recommend a proper cure for the malady."

"Were you making progress in Mona's case?"

"Yes and no." She uncrossed her legs and rose in a graceful motion, walked to a file cabinet and opened a drawer. She pulled out a thick folder and glanced at a few pages in the back of it.

"The last reading evaluation showed that Mona was once again reading at the level of most sixth grade students. That was progress. When she started coming here, she read like a first grader." She put the folder back in the drawer.

"Science aside, what do you think caused Mona's problem?" I asked.

"I can't exclude science," she said. "My opinion is based on what I have learned from asking the right questions."

"And that is?"

"Mona read something that triggered her regression. I don't know if it was something she read prior to the accident or after, but I've narrowed it down to a single item or story, probably a news item or section of a book that caused her to not want to be able to read anything ever again. I was on the verge of getting that out of her when she was killed."

"Thank you for your time, Doctor," I said, rising. "It's been a pleasure meeting you, and I'll keep in touch."

"Please do," she said, giving me that smile that I've never quite been able to figure out. Some women have a way of communicating things with just a smile. I had seen that smile before, many times, but have never quite figured out the meaning.

"If there is a charge for today's discussion, please bill my firm," I said, handing her my card.

CHAPTER THIRTY ONE

I awoke the next morning feeling a compulsion to just forget about the case and take a day off. Call it overload, call it whatever you want. In the past, I've felt myself pushed to the very edge of physical exhaustion while working on cases, and even though this particular case hadn't been as exhausting as some, the fact that I felt I was getting no-where was bugging me. I needed to kick back and do something besides ask questions.

I called Tami and told her that I would probably not see her for a day or two. She didn't question me, but her voice sounded a little sad. She said she'd miss me, but was taking her final bereavement day off from work and planned to clean up the house and decide what to do with Mona's clothes and personal items.

I decided to rent an airboat and some fishing tackle and go fishing. I found a place called Foggy Creek airboat rides in the yellow pages and called them. They had the boats but not the fishing tackle. I found a Bass Pro Shop and asked a very knowledgeable, wizened old salesman what tackle I would need to catch some bass. He sold me $200 worth of tackle, a box and a map to where he assured me the "big" ones were. I took county highway 9336 out of Homestead to a spot south west of Nine Mile Pond and put in to the Hells Bay Canoe Trail. By nine that morning I was whizzing over the Everglades at 30 miles an hour, headed for Bernard Lake, that was the spot on the map where the "big" bass should be. There were a thousand little openings in the grass, all of which might contain some of the "big" ones, but my trusty $6 dollar compass was leading me to the spot where I was assured I would catch some.

I had noticed another boat leave the rental place at about the same time that I left. Once when I slowed to inspect a particularly promising looking spot, I saw the boat go by me, two men waved and I waved back. I resumed my speed and fifteen minutes later I arrived at Bernard Lake. An opening about the size of two football fields side by side. I cut the engine and let the airboat coast over the quiet water until it stopped.

It took me ten minutes to rig a casting reel and tie on the plug that the salesman told me was the best thing he had in stock to catch bass. I made my first cast, a beautiful arching one, and the plug hit the water with a "plunk". I started retrieving the lure, five slow cranks, then a little tug on the end of the rod, five more slow cranks and another tug. Then it hit.

I set the hook and the fight was on. The fish went to my right and away from the boat, the line squealing on the reel drag. I let it run till the squealing stopped and flipped a little switch to set the drag, moved a lever forward, and started to crank. The fish then went left, but not away from me, pulling the tip of the reel from right to left across my body. I cranked hard about five cranks and let up, then watched as the big bass broke water and seemed to walk on its tail towards the boat, shaking its huge head back and forth.

Then it started straight at the boat. I cranked furiously, not wanting it to get under the boat. It veered further left and I cranked some more to take up the slack, then pulled slowly and relentlessly till I had the tip of the rod straight up, then relaxed and cranked as the rod tip descended.

The drag was still letting the fish gain on me so I flipped the lever and set the drag a little tighter. I knew the fish was tiring, and so was I. I estimated it had been five minutes since it hit. I tugged and cranked, tugged and cranked until my arms were sore. Eventually I wore the fish out. It came to the side of the boat and I held the rod with one hand and eased the net down under it with the other. When the net encircled it, the bass gave a final flop and almost jumped out of the net. I had to lay the rod down on the boat and use both hands to lift it in.

It was a beauty.

When I looked up I saw another airboat across the lake from me. It was the one that had passed me earlier with two men who had waved.

"Nice bass," one of them yelled.

"Thanks," I yelled back.

"We're having some engine problems, do you have a cell phone we can use?" One of the men yelled.

"Sure," I said, "Let me secure this fish and I'll be right over."

I put the fish in a tank, dipped some water from the lake and filled the tank, then started the engine. I throttled slow until the boat started moving, then gunned it slightly and sped fifty yards or so towards the other boat before cutting the throttle and letting it coast.

When I pulled even with the other boat one of the men tossed a line and I caught it and pulled my boat up alongside theirs and tied it off.

As I straightened up I saw the gun.

"Put your hands behind your back, don't try anything that'll get you killed."

I have long since learned that Karate cannot stop a speeding bullet, no matter how well you have mastered the fine art of self defense. There's a time when you have to make an instant decision as to whether you want to die or live a while longer, maybe wait for a better stance, closer proximity to the weapon, or find out what is happening. The fact that I wasn't already dead, hadn't been shot yet, factored into the instant decision. Stay alive. Find out what is going down.

I did as I was told. The man who spoke motioned to the other one.

"Cuff him to the prop frame," he said.

The second man, a small, lean man in shorts and tee shirt, snapped cuffs on my left wrist. I heard the short chain rattle as it went around the prop frame, then felt the other end of the cuffs snap around my right wrist.

"Looks like we've caught the biggest fish," the small man said.

"What's going on?" I asked. "Another warning from my arch enemy, Al Sarcosi?"

"Who?" The man with the gun grunted.

I remained silent. If he didn't know Sarcosi, then obviously this wasn't a pay back from the Mafia hood for introducing him to dihydrogen monoxoide.

The man with the gun was dressed in jeans and a long sleeve denim shirt. He wore a straw hat with a chin strap and had the look of someone who had spent years on the water. His face was deeply tanned and had a stubble of beard.

"Who are you, and what do you want with me?"

"We want the lotto ticket," he said.

"What lotto ticket?" I decided to play dumb until I found out what they knew.

"You have it or you know where it is," he said. "We've been following you since that woman was killed. We followed you to the commissioner's office in Tallahassee. Why would you go there if you didn't have the ticket or know where it is?"

"Who are you?" I asked again. "What makes you think I've got the ticket?"

"You've been spending a lot of money, stranger." The skinny one said. "Nobody around here has fancy sports cars and can rent Lincoln Town Cars to drive. That fishing tackle must have cost you at least two hundred. Either you've got that ticket or you know where it is. We want it."

"Shut up, Gene," the older man said. "I'll do the talking."

I glanced back at him. He held the gun on my midsection with his right hand, and motioned towards the west with his left hand.

"We know you and another feller was looking for that goon who owns that raft with a dome on it. We also know that feller is connected somehow to the woman who was killed. Just tell us where the ticket is and we'll let you go."

I didn't believe that for a second. The look in his eyes told me that he'd probably killed a few men in bar room brawls, or left them to drown out in the bay. He just plain looked mean. I'd guess he was an inch or two taller than me, and close to two hundred pounds, broad chest and narrow waist.

"I don't have the ticket, and I don't know where it is. If I did, I wouldn't be here fishing, I'd be vacationing in Hawaii or someplace."

"Or you'd be waiting for the right time to claim it," Gene said.

"Shut up, Gene," the big man said.

"Damn you, Cliff, quit telling me to shut up. You aint got no hold on me, and either we're in this together or I'll take his airboat and go on home."

"Just be quiet and let me think," Cliff said. Gene shut up. I guessed that he felt it was OK to be told to "be quiet" but not "shut up".

"So are you going to shoot me or let me go?" I asked. "I don't have the ticket. I'm a private investigator trying to find out who killed the woman that bought the ticket. I'm working for Charles DuPont."

"That doesn't mean anything to me," Cliff said.

"Do you know DuPont?" I asked.

"Yeah, I've heard of him."

"Then you know that he's a very wealthy man. He's paying me to investigate this case."

"Then what are you doing fishing?"

"I needed some relaxation time. I ran out of questions to ask, so I decided to take a day off and fish. Now will you un-cuff me and let me get back to fishing?"

"Maybe we should take him to Charlie," Gene said.

"Shut up, Gene," Cliff said. "And keep your damned mouth shut. If I want any shit out of you, I'll kick it out."

"Damned you, Cliff," Gene said. "What makes you think I won't just walk away from you and all of this mess. I ain't bound to you."

"Who's Charlie?" I asked, trying to get everything I could out of this situation.

"Keep your mouth shut, Gene," Cliff said, his eyes narrowing.

Whoever Charlie is seemed to play a factor in whether or not I stayed alive. Cliff was hastily trying to keep Gene from saying anything about Charlie.

"What if I let you go? You'll go running back to that policeman, Happs, and tell him I held a gun on you and cuffed you?"

I could sense that Cliff was pondering what to do with me. I felt that he believed me when I told him I didn't have the lotto ticket, and now he had to decide whether to kill me, let me go, or take me to Charlie.

"I don't know you and you haven't hurt me. If you let me go I'll fish till I've caught a half dozen more like that one I just landed and then I'll go back to my motel and forget I ever saw you two."

I could see the wheels turning in Cliff's mind. Of course I favored his second option, to let me go. If he decided to kill me, I had no options. If he decided to take me to Charlie, he was delaying what may be a decision to kill me anyway. But taking me to Charlie was better than killing me here and dumping my body in the Everglades swamp.

"Who is Al Sarcosi?" Cliff asked.

"A man who thinks that he can scare me into stopping my investigation," I said, willing to talk about whatever Cliff asked, to keep from getting shot.

"That name sounds familiar."

"If you knew him, you'd know what I mean," I said.

It wasn't hard for me to see that of the two, Cliff was the one with the brains. He seemed like he had complete control of the situation. I was curious about his background so I asked him about it, trying to buy time and convince him that I knew nothing about the whereabouts of the lotto ticket.

"You seem like you've had some experience in my line of work, Cliff," I said. "Were you an investigator?"

"Not you're kind of investigator," Gene said.

Cliff shot a huge hand out with the speed of a practiced martial arts expert, gathered a handful of Gene's tee shirt and jerked him nearly off his feet.

"I won't tell you again to keep your mouth shut, Gene," he said. "I'll shut it for you."

He released his hold and Gene staggered back, lost his balance and fell off of the boat into the water. He went under and then came back up immediately spitting and sputtering.

"Damn you, Cliff," he said. "Get me out of this water. Don't you know there are gators here?"

"You fell in, you get yourself out," Cliff said, a smile teasing at the corners of his mouth. He thought the sight of Gene falling in the water was comical, and so did I. If I had not been his captive, handcuffed to the engine frame, I would have been slapping my hands on my thighs and roaring with laughter. The gravity of the situation at hand only permitted me to grin instead of laughing out loud.

I watched as Gene grabbed the edge of the boat and pulled himself back aboard, water dripping off his head.

Cliff was still struggling to control his smile.

"What kind of investigator was Cliff, Gene?" I asked.

Gene glared at me and retreated out of Cliff's reach, not seeing the humor of the situation.

"Take them cuffs off of him," Cliff said. "He don't know anything that we don't know. I'm not going to face another jury because of something I didn't do, or something I did do either."

I let that soak in for a minute, thankful that Cliff's decision apparently had been made. I was going to live, for whatever purpose or length of time, I was grateful.

"Are you going to take me to Charlie?" I asked.

"You forget you heard that name," he said. "I'm going to let you go about your fishing. If I see you again I'll probably have to kill you."

"Don't worry," I said. "I have no intention of looking for you two. A lot of people would like to find that lotto ticket, and I can't say as I blame them. You'll get no interference from me." I meant what I said about the lotto ticket. Their complicity in the investigation was a different matter. I knew one thing. If I met the two of them again, I'd have the upper hand.

"How much cash have you got?" Cliff asked.

"Maybe three hundred," I said. "I spent a bundle on this tackle. I'd like to get to use it."

"Get his wallet, Gene."

Gene moved behind me and lifted my wallet. He hadn't yet un-cuffed me. He handed the wallet over to Cliff, who opened it and extracted the bills. He glanced through my identification and left it in the wallet.

"Take the cuffs off," he told Gene.

When the cuffs were off, I rubbed my
wrists and held my hand out towards him.

"Can I have my wallet back?"

He gave it to me.

"Untie your boat," he said. "I hope you
have a nice day fishing, but if you try to
follow us, I'll kill you. No one will ever find
your body out here, alligators will eat you for
lunch."

I believed him.

"Just so we understand each other," I
said, "If I find that either of you have
threatened or harassed Tami Fawn about
that lotto ticket, I'll have to kill you."

He gave me a long, cold look.

"I'm beginning to like the way you
think," he said.

He untied my airboat from theirs and
pushed it away with his foot, still holding the
gun on me. He started the engine on their
boat and shouted one last thing to me.

"Stay here for at least an hour. If you
come after us I'll kill you. Make no mistake
about that."

I believed him again.

CHAPTER THIRTY TWO

I didn't feel much like fishing after they left. Cliff's admonition about staying put for at least an hour was still ringing in my ears, however, so I caught two more nice black bass and a calico, then put my tackle away and cleaned the four fish, packed the meat on ice and drank a beer. I glanced at my watch and saw that only 40 minutes had passed. I used the time to play back everything that had been said while I had been held captive by Gene and Cliff.

Cliff had been an investigator of some sort. He had been to trial for some offense that he felt he was innocent of, and he was working for a man named Charlie. I immediately thought of Charles DuPont. DuPont had mentioned that he had "feelers" out all over the state. Maybe he knew something about Cliff and Gene. I dug out my cell phone and called his home.

His servant answered and put me on hold. After a minute or so he came back on and said that Mr. DuPont could not be disturbed at this time, and asked if there was a message.

"Please ask Mr. DuPont if he would like fresh black bass for dinner," I told him. "Call me back if he does, and I'll bring the fish and some wine."

"Yes, Mr. Yardley," Juan said. "I will call you, please give me your number."

I game him my cell phone number and hung up.

I looked at my watch again and it was 55 minutes from the time Cliff and Gene had left in their boat. I started the engine and thought that if he wanted to kill me over five minutes, then so be it.

I exchanged pleasant talk with the attendant at the airboat rental place, told him I'd caught some nice bass and thanked him for his service.

"By the way, do you happen to know a big guy named Cliff something or other who owns an airboat and may live here in the Everglades?"

"Nope, can't say as I do," he said.

"He hangs out with a little skinny character named Gene. The two of them were fishing the same spot I fished."

"I know a guy named Gene," the attendant said.

I perked up.

"What's he look like?"

"Like a little bit."

"Small man, five six maybe? Thin but wiry looking, long dirty blonde hair?"

"That sounds like Gene."

"Does he live around here?"

"Owns a bait shop around West Lake, at least he used to. I heard he was on drugs for a while and may have sold his shop."

"Got a last name or the name of his bait shop?" I asked.

"Cullen." He said. "I think his shop is called 'Little Shrimp Bait Shop' or something like that."

"Thanks a bunch," I said. "I'll check it out."

"Come back and see us," he smiled.

I had a map of the Everglades Park area in the Lincoln and looked up West Lake. It was not more than twenty miles away so I drove down 9336 and turned south on the road that led towards West Lake. After driving for about three miles I saw a sign that read Shrimpy's Baits 2 miles. That must be it, I thought.

At the bait shop I pulled into a gravel parking lot and parked the car. There was another car in the lot and a battered old Chevy pickup near the back of the twenty by forty foot pole barn structure. I went in, taking my time, looking left and right for any sign of Cliff or Gene. I didn't want to find either one of them without carrying my 9MM with me. At this point I was a little nervous and doubting my decision to drive here to check out Gene Cullen.

A woman was behind the counter. She looked like she might be at least part Seminole Indian. She was tall and thin, very dark. I smiled at her and looked through a glass counter at over-priced fishing lures. She glanced at me but said nothing.

"Gene here?" I finally asked.

"Nope." She said. "Can I help you with something?"

"Naw." I said, trying to sound like I belonged in the area. "Just wanted to gab at him 'bout fishing."

"He'll prob'ly be back after dark, if he can find his way back by then. Prob'ly be drunk."

"OK" I said. "I'll catch him later."

"Can I tell him who asked?"

"I ain't seen him in a while," I said. "I'd like to surprise him."

"OK," she said.

I pretended to look at some fishing equipment, rods and reels, for a few minutes then left. I noticed that she was looking at me from the doorway as I got in the Lincoln and drove away. I knew that if she told Gene a man who drives a Lincoln was looking for him, Gene would know it was me. Then he would tell Cliff, and they might come looking for me. I decided that if they did they might get more than they bargained for, and my heart revved up a few beats, thinking that I don't like being threatened, handcuffed to motor frames, and told to mind my own business.

My business is investigating and that's what I intended to do, warning or no warning.

If Alfredo Sarcosi couldn't scare me, I felt that the Cliff and Gene duo wasn't going to hamper my investigation at all.

CHAPTER THIRTY THREE

My cell phone rang just as I started in the door to the Homestead Police Headquarters building. I made a U turn in the foyer and went back outside and answered it.

"Mr. Yardley," it was Juan, Charles DuPont's manservant.

"Yes, Juan."

"Mr. DuPont has instructed me to tell you to drop the fish off at his gate at 5 this evening. I'll be waiting. Return at 6:30. I'll prepare the fish. He said that he prefers a light wine with fish, but the choice is yours."

"Thank you, Juan," I said, and hung up. It was nearly 4:00 now and I'd have to make my visit with Detective Happs a fast one. Happs didn't know I was coming in, and I might not even find him in his office.

But I did.

We shook hands and he asked me to sit down.

"Do you know anything about dihydrogen monoxide?" he asked.

I grinned.

"Sarcosi?"

"I thought I told you to stay away from him, Yardley." His voice wasn't rough, as a matter of fact there was a slight hint of humor in it. "You're going to keep on until either Sarcosi rubs you out or I run you in."

"You heard about that?"

"Yes, I did, as a matter of fact," he said, trying hard not to grin.

"Would you like to hear why I did that?"

"Lets hear it," he said. "It's not going to change my warning to you to stay away from Sarcosi, but I'll listen."

"Three of his goons jumped me in a mall parking lot. One of them even tried to shoot me. Your boys were there, I saw the squad cars right after it happened."

"That was you?" His mouth opened and his jaw dropped.

"In person," I said.

"Witnesses say you beat the shit out of all three of them, including the guy with the gun." He seemed astonished.

"Well I wouldn't go so far as to say that," I said. "It was strictly self defense on my part. Contrary to whatever your witnesses say, I just tried to get away from the situation."

"Damned you, Yardley," he said, but I could tell by his voice that he wasn't as mad as he pretended to be. "You're gonna keep it up till something dreadful happens to you, then I'll have another murder case on my hands. Can't you just forget about Sarcosi?"

"Sure, as long as he forgets about interfering with my investigation," I told him. "And that brings me to the reason I am here. What do you know about a man named Cliff who might have been an investigator of some kind and was tried for something he didn't do, acquitted, but lost his job?"

"Cliff Stone?" he asked.

"I didn't get his surname."

"What about him?"

"Him and a man named Gene Cullen held a gun on me, cuffed me to the engine frame on an airboat, and threatened to kill me."

"When did all that happen?"

"Today. I was out fishing, minding my own business. I needed a day off from working this Mona Fawn case," I said. "They wanted the lotto ticket. I convinced them I didn't have it and had no idea where it was. Has it surfaced yet?"

"Not to my knowledge," he said. "So Cliff is looking for the lotto ticket? It would be your word against his that he held a gun on you and cuffed you. That's paramount to kidnapping in this state. Cliff's not one to take that charge lightly."

"Who is he?" I asked.

"Clifford Stone, formerly with the Federal Bureau of Investigation."

"FBI?" I whistled.

"Yeah. He was working undercover on a drug bust here in Miami. He had nearly got to the top of a major supplier when things went sour. Miami police didn't know that he was on the case and were doing an investigation of their own. When they kicked down the door to a motel room where Cliff was questioning a suspect, they found the suspect dead, Cliff standing over him with a smoking gun."

"Cliff didn't shoot the suspect?"

"Claims he didn't. He said there were two persons in the room other than himself. He said the other man in the room shot the victim, and that he, Cliff, scuffled with the other man, took the gun away from him just as the Miami boys kicked down the door. The third person exited through a door to an adjoining room and escaped."

"And a jury believed him?"

"Actually, no. They convicted him of manslaughter."

"How'd he get out?"

"A technicality. It seems that when the Miami boys found out Cliff was an undercover FBI agent, they forgot to read him his rights. A federal judge overturned the conviction. Cliff quit the bureau, worked a while for the Miami force, then got fired for hitting the bottle."

"He's an alcoholic?"

"Not really. I think it was more than the bottle he hit. Story I got is that he knocked the chief of police on his ass and walked away. No charges were filed for assault, but the chief fired Cliff."

"Do you know what that was all about?"

"I heard that the chief caught Cliff nipping at a bottle from his desk and chewed him out good. Cliff said that as long as he was taking an ass chewing for drinking, he might as well finish it. He turned the bottle up and drank it down. The chief called him an irresponsible drunk and Cliff hit him."

"How about Gene Cullen? Any thing on him?"

"Gene was an attorney. He represented Cliff in the trial for manslaughter. He was later dismissed from the bar for a drug problem. He opened a bait shop down in the 'glades and went to a clinic. I heard he's back on drugs again, but I don't know that to be a fact."

"Gene let it slip that they might want to take me to a man named Charlie," I said. "I thought they might be referring to Charles DuPont, but I doubt it. I'm having dinner with DuPont tonight, and I'll ask him, but do you have any idea who this "Charlie" might be?"

"Nope." He said. "Do you want to press charges on these birds?"

"No," I said. "I've got nothing to back my claim. Like you said, it would be their word against mine, and there was two of them. I'll wait till I get more on them and I'll tell you about it when I do."

"Well, I'm still upset at your game with Sarcosi," he said. "I wouldn't have known about that unless one of my men told me. He went there to eat and found the place closed. He knows Al and went to see him. Al told him that he'd been shut down by the city because of something called dihydrogen monoxide. My man laughed in his face. Pissed old Al off terrible, and when he found out it was a hoax, he got so mad he threatened to kill you."

"His goons tried that," I said. "I imagine he'll try again. Next time, though, I'm packing an equalizer. I'm getting too old to defend against three guys at one time."

"I could take your permit to carry away from you," he said.

"Get a court order and you can have my gun," I told him. "Without one, you and your entire force can't take it away from me."

"Don't be so damned arrogant, Yardley," he said. "I was just beginning to enjoy your antics and now you are trying to piss me off."

"I don't mean to do that," I said hastily. "What I'm saying is this. Anything I do is self defense. I'm sure that a judge will listen to my side about carrying if I tell them about Sarcosi's thugs trying to shoot me. I've got witnesses to that, including your own response team."

"OK." he said. "You win the battle, just don't lose the war."

I stood up and stuck out my hand. "Friends?" I asked.

He shook hands with me and smiled. "I'd rather be your friend than your enemy."

CHAPTER THIRTY FOUR

I stopped at an expensive wine dealer and bought a good bottle of Gewürztraminer, took it and the fish to Juan at Charles DuPont's front gate, then drove back to the motel for a shower.

I swam in the motel pool for twenty minutes, showered and dressed and was back at DuPont's front gate by the appointed time. I buzzed the gate and Juan let me in.

DuPont invited me to join him in his study for a drink while Juan finished preparing dinner. He was dressed in a pair of white gabardine slacks and a blue and gray pull over shirt. White tennis shoes, the old fashioned cloth kind, were on his feet.

"Do you have anything to report regarding your investigation?" He asked.

"Probably nothing you don't already know," I told him. "I've been working on it, but I took a day off and caught some fish this morning, I thought you might enjoy them."

"Thank you," he said. "The investigation is going smoothly?"

"Yes, I've learned a lot," I said. "If you'd like I can have my office mail you what I know as of today, but I'll tell you now if you prefer a verbal account."

I had been calling in a report daily to a voicemail box and had left instructions to have someone type everything and put it in a file. Every move I had made, including the trip to Alfredo Sarcosi's deli was on file in my office.

"Your personal account would be nice," he said.

I started. I told him everything I had done since I had seen him last, with the exception of the fishing trip and the visit to Happs. He sat quietly, listening. If he had any questions he kept them to himself. When I finished he looked at me and spoke quietly.

"You've disobeyed my instructions."

That took me momentarily by surprise.

"In what way?"

"In two ways, Kip," he said. "First, you have continued to play tic-tac-toe with Sarcosi. I warned you about that. Secondly, you have taken an interest in my great granddaughter that violates our agreement. You were told that she is off limits to your personal life. That doesn't sit well with me."

"Let's get something straight, Mr. DuPont," I said. "I'm not one of your house servants. I do not take orders from you. Our agreement is that I would try to find out who caused the plane wreck that killed your daughter and son-in-law, and to find the person or persons responsible for the death of you granddaughter, Mona. Other than that, I owe you nothing. My personal life is my own, and if Tami doesn't want to see me again, then she can tell me that. Not you, or anyone else, can control my personal life."

I got up, walked to the door and turned back to face him.

"Enjoy the fish, Mr. DuPont," I said.

"Sit down, Kip," he said in a soft tone. "You called me about dining with me. Let's be civil about this. We'll have a nice meal and forget our differences about Tami. I apologize if I've seemed controlling."

I hesitated. He had got to a spot that few people have ever reached without dire consequences. He had interfered in my personal decision making, a place where I'm very sensitive, a place that rubs against the very fiber of my personality. Not since I was a teenager under the restraints of a domineering, abusive stepmother, have I let anyone control me.

"As long as we understand each other," I said. "And I apologize if I seem rude."

I sat down and stared at the ceiling for a moment.

We remained silent until he offered me another drink and I politely declined.

"What do you know about a former FBI agent, named Cliff Stone and his sidekick, a bait shop owner named Gene Cullen?" I asked, to melt the ice.

"I read the account in the newspapers about Stone," he said. "Gene Cullen was a mouthpiece for the mob. He represented Sarcosi's son in a hit and run trial that was summarily dismissed when the prosecuting attorney backed off. How do they fit in your investigation?"

"I'm not sure they have any connection," I said. "They are looking for the lotto ticket, not the killer."

He didn't say anything.

"The name "Charlie" came up while talking to Cliff Stone. I thought you might have some connection to the two."

"I have no connection," he said. "I'm seldom referred to as "Charlie". Everyone who knows me calls me "Charles" or "Chuck". No-one calls me "Charlie". I don't like that name. It sounds like a child's nickname to me."

"Do you know anyone named "Charlie"?" I asked.

"I know a lot of people, Kip," he said. "I'm sure that there are a few acquaintances or people that I've met who go by that name. The one I can think of immediately is my daughter's father in law, Carlos Fawn. Some people called him "Charlie" before he disappeared."

"When did he disappear?" I asked, although I thought I knew the answer.

"Right after the funeral for his son and my daughter," DuPont answered. "His grief made some think that he went out in the 'glades and took his own life."

"Do you think that?"

"No. I knew Carlos before his son married my daughter. He wasn't the type that would commit suicide."

"If he is still living, why do you think he remains reclusive?"

"Fear." He said. "He probably knows something about Harold and Harriet's death, something that will get him killed, or worse, if he tells it. I'd be very interested in finding Carlos, myself. Of course I wouldn't kill him if he didn't give me the information that I want, but someone may want him dead to keep that information from surfacing."

"Why didn't you bring that up when you gave me the folder on the accident?" I asked.

"Carlos could be dead already," he said. "And if he isn't dead, he could be anywhere. He hasn't been seen or heard of around here for nearly 40 years but that doesn't mean he's dead. On the other hand, this is a big country, Kip. Carlos could be anywhere, in any state. Hell, he may even be out of the States, Puerto Rico or Mexico or somewhere."

"Was Fawn a Cuban?" I asked, wondering just what bloodline the name Fawn represented.

"No, his mother was from Mexico, his father a Native American, Seminole. Carlos knew the everglades better than any man I've ever known. He could have survived all these years in the swamps. His father lived off of alligators and fish, and Carlos grew up in the 'glades."

"I think I'll rustle the bushes a little and see if I can find out who "Charlie" is," I said.

"How do you propose doing that?"

"I'm going to pay a visit to Gene Cullen. He was one of two men who held a gun on me today and demanded that I give them the lotto ticket."

"What?" he said, "Someone thought you had the ticket?"

I told him about the incident on Bernard Lake.

"And the other man was Cliff Stone?" he asked.

"Yes."

"How do you plan to make Gene Cullen talk to you? He's not the most reliable mouthpiece. His reputation as an attorney is cloudy at best. He made most of his money representing crooks and drug dealers."

"Rumor has it that he is using drugs," I said. "Maybe I can bait him a bit. Chumming is the expression a fisherman would use."

At that point Juan appeared as if by magic and informed my host that dinner was ready. We had a great meal and I thanked

Charles DuPont for his hospitality and left. His admonition about seeing Tami made me want to see her.

I called her and told her that I would like to see her. She seemed glad that I called and wanted to know if I had eaten. When I told her that I had dinner with Charles DuPont, she said merrily, "OK. I'll fix a desert and we can have a glass of wine."

"I'll be there in a half an hour," I said.

CHAPTER THIRTY FIVE

Early the next morning I drove back to Shrimpy's Bait Shop and talked to the dark-skinned woman again. She seemed a little more willing to talk than my previous visit, even smiled a couple of times. I got the impression that she didn't particularly like her job, but didn't have much choice.

"How long have you worked here?" I asked, casually.

"Too damned long," she said, grinning. "I hired on the day they opened this place."

"Did Gene Cullen hire you?"

"Yep," she said, brushing her dark hair away from her face. "He said he'd give me a raise after six months. It's been a lot longer than that, and I ain't seen a raise yet. I'd quit but I've got kids that'd go hungry."

"You have young children?" I asked, glancing at her. She appeared to be in her mid fifties, and I was curious about a woman that age having young children.

"Grandkids," she said. "I support them. One is thirteen, the other nine. I have to leave them at home by themselves while I work, and sometimes the older one doesn't watch the younger one. I'm afraid the child welfare people will take them. That would kill me."

"Where can I find Gene this morning?" I asked, changing the subject.

"Probably at home sleeping," she said. "He doesn't show up here until noon or so."

"I guess I could wake him up," I said. "Can you tell me how to find his house?"

"I'd have to draw you a map," she said. "The way out to his place is confusing, because of the waterways and the swamp. I'll draw you a map."

I waited while she got a piece of paper and a pencil from under the counter and laboriously drew a sketch on it. She was a lot smarter than I had assumed. The map was painstakingly detailed, she had drawn an arrow with the letter "N" at the top and another with the letter "S" at the bottom.

"Would I be able to find the place using my GPS in my car?" I asked her.

"I doubt it," she said. "Some of these roads have never been added to a map. If you don't know they are there you'd never find them."

I glanced at the map again to see if there were any questions I might ask. I noticed she had written "approx. 4 miles" from the bait shop to the first turn I'd have to make.

"Thank you very much," I said. "I don't even know your name, but I'd like to pay you for your trouble."

"My name's Consuela," she said. "You don't have to pay me. I didn't ask for any money."

I hauled out my wallet and extracted one of the ten twenty dollar bills that I had got from an ATM to replace the money Cliff and Gene had taken. I placed it on the counter.

"Thanks again," I said, and left.

I found the first turn without any difficulty. She was right, there was no marker or sign designating the name of the road. It turned south off of the gravel road and about a half mile later, curved east. I glanced at the map and saw that my next turn would be a right, south again. Consuela had written "abt. 2 mi." so I watched the odometer. At nearly exactly two miles, I saw a small road, not much larger than two tire paths wide. I turned the Lincoln right and slowed my speed, the ground beneath the tires still seemed firm enough but I was concerned that I'd get stuck if I got out of the tire tracks I was following.

The road had been graveled but grass had grown up down the middle and had not been mowed in quite some time. It twisted and turned several times and I saw the edge of the water within fifteen feet of the road, cattails and saw grass growing profusely. I turned off on similar roads, following the map for ten minutes.

As I neared the spot indicated by a box with an "X" in it, I slowed and parked the Lincoln on a 10 by 20 foot patch of gravel. Ahead of me was a log home, nicely shaped, built up on a platform supported by several railroad ties. The house was constructed of logs, assembled to resemble an old fashioned log home, not large, I guessed it was probably two bedrooms and one bath.

I got out of the Lincoln and approached the house carefully looking for signs of life. All of the window shades were down in front of the house, I saw no movement to indicate that anyone was stirring.

I walked up on the porch and knocked on the screen door, rattling it against the frame, and waited. No one answered so I tried again. I heard the sound of someone grumbling something and the soft shuffling of feet towards the door. The door opened two inches and two pale blue eyes looked out at me.

"What do you want?"

"I'd like to speak to Gene if I may," I said.

"He's sleeping," the voice said. "Come back around 10."

"I can't do that," I said. "I'm from out of town and I have to leave soon."

"Who are you?"

"Just an old friend from law school," I said. "I borrowed some money from Gene and I'd like to pay it back. Are you his wife?"

That was a ruse that often worked. When someone thinks there is money involved, they will take measures that they otherwise would not take.

"Just a minute," she said.

I heard the shuffling sound as she walked away, then a door opened somewhere in the interior of the cabin.

"Gene," I heard her yell. "Some guy's here. He wants to pay you back some money."

I heard more grumbling and a few four letter words. Then heavier footsteps approaching the door. I moved slightly to the side so that my face wouldn't be seen immediately. I saw Gene approaching, dressed in a Florida Gators tee shirt and a pair of Sponge Bob under shorts.

When he opened the door I jerked the screen door open and stepped in fast, pushing him away from the door.

I had my 9MM in my hand.

"Don't make any noises, Gene," I said. "We're going for a ride."

"What the hell?" he said

"You heard me," I grabbed his arm, pushed the barrel of the 9MM against his ribs. "Just do as I say and I won't blow you away. Now lets walk."

"Let me get some clothes on," he said.

"No time," I said. "Walk!"

He walked with me, I opened the passenger door of the car and pushed him in, and put the 9MM back in my waistband.

I got in and started the engine.

"You'll be sorry for this," he promised. "Cliff will cut you to pieces and feed your ass to the gators."

"We'll see," I said.

I reversed the directions Consuela had given me, drove back past the bait shop and up the road to 9336 and turned right. I had passed a cheap motel on the way down and it fit in with my plan. When I found it again, I turned in and told Gene to get out.

"We're going to rent a room, Gene," I said. "If you say one word it may be your last."

I pushed him ahead of me toward the rental office and picked up a plastic Wal-Mart bag from the back seat that contained a fifty foot length of quarter inch nylon rope.

A sleepy clerk looked up as we went in.

"Can we get a room?" I asked.

The clerk looked at us like we were crazy. He glanced at Gene's Sponge Bob under shorts and then at me

"How long do you want it for?" he asked.

"As long as it takes," I said, winking at him.

He frowned and pushed a ledger towards me. I signed two fictitious names and put a hundred dollars on the counter.

"If it's more than that, I'll pay you with a credit card," I said. "We probably won't be more than a day or two."

He gave me a key and pointed to the left down the row of rooms. "Number Four," he said. "Fourth one on your left."

He took the money and put it in a drawer under the counter, looked at me with knowing eyes and winked back at me.

"Have a good time," he said.

Gene had remained perfectly silent like he was told, but I wasn't sure how long he would keep quiet. In the room I took the rope and tied Gene's hands behind his back, then tied them to the doorknob of the bathroom door.

"We can make this quick or we can take our time," I said. "What I want is some names, Gene. How many names you give me will determine how long I keep you here. I'll gag you if I have to but for now I'll forget the gag."

I could see his nostrils flare and he looked at me with a stare that told me he was already worried. Sweat appeared suddenly across his brow.

"There's a plus side to this," I said. "You tell me what I want to know, and I'll give you what you want."

I took a plastic sandwich bag from my pocket, dumped the white powder out a little at a time on the dresser top, and dropped a soda straw near it.

"This is what you want, isn't it Gene?"

He nodded, licking his lips, staring at the white powder.

"Who is Charlie?"

He was silent. I saw a glimpse of fear in his eyes, but there was something else. It was resolve. This might take longer than I imagined.

"This is good stuff," I said. "Cost me a bundle. It's all yours, Gene, all you have to do is co-operate a little."

"Martha has already probl'y called Cliff," he told me. "Cliff will find me. You'll wish you'd never seen me."

"Martha probably went back to bed, Gene. We can make this a lot more uncomfortable," I said. "I can take you back to Bernard Pond and dangle your legs in the water. I might even cut a couple of slices across your shins, just enough to bleed. Gators like the smell of blood, don't they?"

"You wouldn't do that," he said. "You ain't got it in you."

"Don't be too sure of that," I said. "Now who is Charlie, and where can I find him?"

"Go to hell," he said.

I sat on the edge of the bed and flicked on an old TV set, tuned it to Andy of Mayberry and watched. I glanced at my watch. It was just eight o'clock. I made a bet with myself that Gene would break before noon.

I watched the thirty minute episode where Barney inadvertently lets the crooks lock him in a cell. When it was over, I took a credit card from my wallet, separated a small pile of the white powder from the rest and scooted it around until I had I nice line about five inches long and a quarter of an inch wide.

"It's here waiting for you, Gene," I said. "Who is Charlie?"

Silence. I watched another thirty minute episode of Andy of Mayberry.

"I can put this back in the bag or I can take it in the bathroom and flush it down the toilet," I said, watching his face carefully.

"You son-of-a" he started to call me a name I do not like and I stepped close and slapped him across the lips, drawing blood.

"Naughty, naughty, Gene," I said. "You're making this a lot harder than it needs to be. Just tell me who Charlie is and where to find him, and I'll untie you and walk out of here. You can do the whole bag before you call Cliff. Wouldn't that be nice? The whole bag, all to yourself, Gene."

He spit blood on the floor and looked hard and long at the line of white powder on the dresser. I knew he was on the verge of telling me what I wanted to hear, I just needed a key phrase to say, something that would be the last push.

I thought about the entire scenario. What would I want most if I was in Gene's shoes? Aside from the white powder, he probably wanted a drink of water.

I picked up a plastic covered glass from the dresser and unwrapped it and filled it with water from the bathroom sink. I stood in front of Gene and drank it slowly. His eyes looked at me, pleading.

"Thirsty?" I asked.

"Yeah, give me a drink of water."

"Sure," I said. I refilled the glass and held it to his lips for a second. He took a swallow, nearly choked, but got it down and drank again. I took the glass away and poured the rest of it down the front of his Gator tee shirt.

"Who is Charlie?" I asked, for the umpteenth time.

He told me.

When I had all the details that I wanted, names, places, addresses, I untied his hands from the bathroom door knob, left the pile of talcum powder on the dresser and left, taking the soda straw with me. He was madly scrambling around trying find something to roll into a straw when I started the Lincoln and drove away. He was going to hate me.

CHAPTER THIRTY SIX

Charlie Cervato was not hard to find. He lived in a small concrete block home on the south side of Homestead. I don't know who was more surprised, Charlie or I, when I rang his doorbell and he came to the door and I said, "Carlos Fawn?"

He turned a pale shade of bronze.

"No, Senor," he said. "You've got the wrong address."

"I don't think so, Carlos," I said. "I've went to a lot of trouble to find you, and what I have to say may be worth it. I just want to talk to you for a few minutes. My name is Kip Yardley, I'm a private investigator. May I come in?"

He backed away from the door slowly, both hands held defensively in front of his lean, muscular body. His hair was still very black, his eyes blacker, and his skin the color of English walnuts. He appeared to be in very good shape for his age, that I guessed to be in his late eighties.

I followed him into the room, a sparsely furnished small living room. On one side was a twin sized bed, unmade. On the other side was an old blue recliner facing a small television set. Carlos sat on the edge of the bed.

"How'd you find me?" he asked.

"That's not important," I said. "But keep this in mind, if I found you, so can anyone. All it takes is one slip of the tongue by anyone you trust, and those you don't trust will be able to track you down."

"Sarcosi send you?"

That was something I didn't expect to hear, but now that I'd heard it, pieces started falling in to place. The only thing wrong was the place they were falling. I had it pegged wrong. I thought that Sarcosi and Carlos Fawn were working together, they had both been minor players in the mob.

"No one sent me," I said. "You've got nothing to fear from me."

"What do you want?" he asked.

"Information. First, why have you remained hidden from society for the past thirty years? What is it you are afraid of? You wouldn't have deserted Mona if you weren't afraid of something."

"It didn't help," he said sadly. "They got Mona instead of me. God I wish it had been me. I should have quit when it would have done some good. It's too late now."

"Who got Mona?" I asked. "Do you know who killed your granddaughter?"

"No," he said, touching a handkerchief to his eyes. "If I knew, he'd be a dead man now, turning to *caca* in the belly of a gator. I'll get the sonofabitch that did it!"

"What is it you know that has you so spooked you've kept it locked inside all this time?"

"I don't *know* anything," he said. "It is what I suspect that has been my secret. I can't give you names. I just have some things that I should have told the cops about when my boy was killed."

"You think Harold was killed?"

"I'm sure of it," he said. "It was what he knew that I suspected."

"Tell me about it," I said softly. "I'm not your enemy. I'm working for Tami and Charles DuPont."

"You went to see Sarcosi, my sources told me that."

"He's tied up in this someway," I said.

"I believe he was the one who killed my son."

"Then let me help," I said. "We are on the same side. I want to find Mona's killer as much as you do, and Charles DuPont is footing my bill. He's got the money, so why not let him foot the bill? Just confide in me, and we'll be on the same team."

"That was always a problem," he said slowly.

"Can you elaborate on that?"

"Harry developed the software for the Florida Lotto," Carlos said. "Then he was asked to go to New York to talk to some old friends of mine, they tried to buy him. You know the Mafia controls the lotto. The states say that they control it, but that's a crock of *caca*. It's the mob that really controls it."

"So Harry had something the mob wanted," I said, prompting him.

"No. Harry wouldn't do something the mob wanted him to do. He refused to program the computers so that the mob could make the drawings come out to their best interest."

"But you just said he went there to talk to them. What was it they wanted to talk about?"

Carlos took a long look at the floor, glanced at me and said, "All Harry wanted was a cut of the mob's take on a fair system. I'm the one who clued him in that the Florida lotto was ran by the mob. He had already contracted with the state to design the program. His program handled the financial end of the gambling. It had nothing to do with the drawing of the numbers, the winner or the outcome."

"So it didn't matter to Harry that the mob was the big winner, no matter who the held the winning ticket?"

"Harry was a practical man, Yardley," he said. "I taught him from the time he was a child that there are some things a man can control and some things a man has no control over. I taught him to take advantage of the things he could control in his life, and not to sweat the rest."

"That didn't set well with the mob?"

"It didn't set well with a lot of people, including his father-in-law, Charles DuPont."

"I was from the other side of the tracks. My father was a brick layer, a Seminole who migrated to Mexico. I was brought up with brick dust in my veins and the attitude that if I had a chance to get something for my labors to take it. Different strokes for different folks."

"Harry took after his mother. He believed that the game was fair. When he refused to play the game crooked, it cost him his life."

"How could he have changed the game?"

"I don't know." He said. "I'm not a computer whiz. But if it could be done, Harry could do it."

"Did you have any contact with Harry after he talked to the New York people?" I asked.

"Harry called me from the airport where he refueled in Georgia. He said the big boys had offered him a lot of money. I suspect that the offer itself was the reason Harry was killed. The New York mob was afraid that Harry would blow the whistle, upsetting their apple cart in Florida, where they were the true financial winners in the state lotto."

"Can you explain that?"

"No." He sighed, getting up and walking to the door. He looked out the window like he was expecting someone to arrive. "All of the money doesn't go towards education, and all of it doesn't go to the winners. There are ways to siphon off money, otherwise the mob wouldn't have pushed so hard to get the lotto started in the first place. It's like a legalized numbers system. When I was a young man the numbers racket was ran by the mob, they just upgraded it to lotto. Now they control every lotto in every state. I can't prove that, but it's my guess."

"Wouldn't state inspectors have to get involved?"

"I'm sure they did," he said. "But maybe they're being bought off."

"What else did Harry say to you the night he called from the Georgia airport?"

"He said that his wife was going to fly back with him. She had been to New York on a shopping spree and was ready to return. She cancelled her airline ticket and decided to fly back with Harry. They had argued about the plane Harry bought and she wanted to make up so she decided to fly home with him."

I was silent for a few minutes, trying to think if there was anything else that Carlos might know that would help me in my investigation. He might have learned something from his association with Cliff and Gene. I decided to ask.

"I'll tell you how I found you, but be careful how you answer. Whatever you tell me, I'm bound by law to report to the authorities at some point. If you don't want them to know, don't tell me. O.K."

"I don't want anyone to know I'm alive!" he said. "I've got a handful of friends who I trust. Other than that, I've managed to remain alive by keeping my mouth shut. You know everything that I know."

"How do Cliff Stone and Gene Cullen fit in to this?"

"Ah. I see. That's how you found me. I thought I could trust that pair."

"How did you get tangled up with them?" I asked.

"I knew Cliff's father. We worked as bricklayers together. He's dead now, but before he died he told me that if I ever needed help to get in touch with Cliff, since Cliff was studying to be an FBI agent. I found Cliff after he stood trial. Gene Cullen was cliff's attorney. For some reason Cliff thought he could use Cullen so I agreed to hire him too, to try to find the missing lotto ticket. We decided that with that money all three of us could put our lives back on track. I want to use it to get revenge on the ones who killed my son and granddaughter. Cliff wants it to go after the drug lords that caused his grief, and Gene wants it to kick his habit and get his practice back."

"What about Tami?" I asked. "Wouldn't the ticket belong to her?"

"Tami has a good life," he said. "She's a well educated professional, and her other great grandfather will see that she never wants for anything. I would share with her, too."

He looked at me then, a question making his brow wrinkle.

"Was it Cliff and Gene who led you to me? I thought I could trust those two with my life."

"Actually it was Gene," I told him. I recounted the fishing trip, the few slips that Gene had made, and how I had tricked Gene into talking by using talcum powder for cocaine.

"He'll want to take your head off for that," he said. "But good for you. He needs someone to watch him all of the time, and that is what Cliff was doing. Gene has information on drug lords and mafia members," he said. "Cliff had an interest in keeping Gene clean. Gene will thank you one day for what you did, even though right now he'd like to kill you probably."

"Where did he get the money to open the bait shop?"

"I backed him."

"So you really own the bait shop?"

"You could say that," he offered. "It's in my name."

"Did you know Gene promised Consuela a raise but never delivered on his promise?"

"You mean she didn't get the extra money I budgeted for her raise?"

"She told me she hadn't had a raise."

"That little sonofabitch," he said under his breath. "I'll see that she gets a raise. We were pretty close after the death of my wife, years ago. I owe her."

"Thanks," I told him. "And thanks for the information. I've learned a lot. I don't have all the answers yet, but believe me, I'm going to find out who killed your son, and who killed Mona."

"I believe you will," he told me.

CHAPTER THIRTY SEVEN

I wanted to talk to ValJean Dupont. I drove down to the marina where I had first laid eyes on his strange dome raft to see if he had returned. No such luck.

I asked the attendant in the office if he had heard from ValJean.

"Not a word. It's not like him to stay gone this long without getting in touch. He always worried about a storm coming up and he wanted us to know where he and his raft were."

I got back in the Lincoln and drove to a shady spot in the marina, parked and got my cell phone. I got information and asked for Conch's souvenir shop and dialed the number. It buzzed a few times before being answered.

"Conch's souvenir's," a voice said. It sounded like the woman I had bought the key chain from.

"Hello lovely lady," I said, in my warmest voice.

"Well, hello," she said, "Did you find the dome people?"

I was hoping she would remember me, and she had.

"Yes, but not the particular person I was looking for," I said. "Maybe you would know him. He's about six feet tall, walks with a slight limp because of a prosthetic leg, and is rather heavy set. Dark hair, dark eyes."

"Oh I know who you mean," she said. "He stops here once in a while and buys date milk shakes. I don't know his name, but it has to be the same man."

"When was the last time he was in?" I asked.

"Well let me think, I'm not real sure about that."

"Was it after I was there looking for him?"

She was silent a minute. I thought I'd lost my connection. I looked at the phone. Then I heard her saying something. I put the phone back to my ear quickly.

"....but I think it was," she was saying.

"I'm sorry, I missed that, a little dead space on the line, I guess. Would you repeat that?"

"I said I think it was before you were here," she told me. "Let me ask my stock boy. He sometimes gets in long winded talks with that fella. I have to keep telling him to get back to work."

I heard her asking someone if they'd seen the man with the wooden leg lately. Then she came back on the line.

"Nope," she said. "It must have been before you were here."

"OK, lovely lady," I said. "You've helped me a lot. I'll stop and see you next time I'm up that way."

"Do that, kiddo," she said.

I hung up and called Spencer Adams, the man who had helped me with the spoof about dihydrogen monoxide with Al Sarcosi.

"Hello, Spence," I said after he answered. "Would you have time to fly me back down the coast again. I still haven't found our friend, ValJean DuPont."

"I was just thinking about that," he said. "I'll call you back in a few minutes. I've had some mechanics doing a yearly check on my plane. If they are finished, no problem. I'll call them and find out."

"OK," I said. "Thanks, Spence. I owe you."

"You don't owe me anything," he said. "I still have a dog in this hunt too. I'm still interested in making those dome rafts."

I had hung up the phone when it rang in my hand before I could put it back in my pocket.

"Hello."

"Kip Yardley?"

"Yes. Who's calling?"

"Can't you see, it is me."

I hadn't looked at the number, and didn't recognize the voice right away.

"Richard Rheames?"

"Live and in living color," he said, laughing.

Richard had a way of saying things that have nothing to do with the conversation at hand, off of the wall things and rhyming ramblings, like 'see you later alligator'.

"What's up, Richard?"

"I've got a little info for you," he said. I was suddenly very intent on what he was saying. I'd nearly forgotten about the photograph I had sent him.

"You identified the valve?"

"Not quite," he told me. "Not much to go on there, teddy bear. When will you be back in LA? This is going to cost you at least two ball games, one Dodger game and one Angel game."

Each time Richard found a bit of information for me he held it at ransom until I agreed to go to a ball game with him. After my divorce and while I was still living in the Long Beach area, we had gone to a few games.

"OK, Richard," I said. "What've you got?"

"It is a standard fuel shut off valve. It has been modified, however. There is an adapter at the top of the valve that has been added. We were able to determine the purpose of the adapter by running a composite picture through our data base. It appears to be some sort of radio receiver. I'd say this particular valve could have been controlled from a distance of two or three miles, remotely."

"You could tell all of that?" I asked, amazed.

"Not absolutely," he said. "Does that help?"

"Well, I had already determined that much," I said, "I'm amazed that you could learn that from studying the picture. Do you have anything else?"

"There were two letters and a number that showed under high resolution microscopic enhancement on the receiver unit. The numbers aren't important to you, Scooby Doo, but we've traced the manufacturer of the radio device to a company that makes model airplanes."

"Model airplanes?"

"Yeah, you know, the kind you fly remotely from the ground?"

"OK," I said, my breath coming a little faster.

"They were designed to be used on a particular model airplane that was sold to hobby shops on the east coast. The manufacturer told me that none have ever been sold anywhere except Georgia and Florida. They quit making that model twenty years ago, though."

"Richard, can you fax me printouts of all the information? I'm right in the middle of something and expecting another call. I owe you two ballgames, and thanks a bunch."

"Sure, Kip," he said. "Where should I send the stuff, powder puff?"

I gave him the fax number of the library where I had been doing my research.

"I'll get on it right now," he said.

"Thanks, Richard," I said and hung up.

It was a short drive to the library, but by the time I got there the faxes had arrived. The librarian on duty had been friendly to me and recognized me when I walked through the door.

"Mr. Yardley," she said. "I have some faxes here for you that just arrived."

"Thank you," I told her, taking the papers and heading for my favorite table. I spread the papers out on the table and glanced through them. I found the one with the name of the company that had made the model airplane that used the receiver. It was the receiver itself that I was interested in, but then I needed to digest the information in all of the papers. I read through each page carefully. The model that had used that particular receiver was a XM15. It was a large model that resembled a P51 Mustang.

I went back to the main desk and asked the friendly librarian if she could point me to a book or magazine that featured model airplane flying clubs in the area during the time frame of the crash of Harold Fawn's aircraft. She led me to a section that held books on hobbies of all sorts, then narrowed it down to models, before leaving me on my own.

I fumbled through the books, taking them out one at a time, leafing through them and replacing them in the spot where they belonged. One of them caught my eye. It had the title: "Florida Flying Federation" with the large letters F-F-F formed by a group of people on the ground, each holding a transmitter, pointed to the sky. I pulled the book out and opened it to the index. I ran my finger down the index of the book, looking for anything that jumped out at me, and soon found it.

When I got the letter "H" in the alphabetical index, there was a chapter with the title "Homestead Model Aircraft Flying Club" on page 166. I opened the book to 166 and stood there reading down the list of members. Next to each member's name was a small picture and a brief blurb about that person's performance in the club.

Under "D" I found Dupont, ValJean. The picture of him was as a young man. I read the blurb. "ValJean Dupont, the youngest of the qualified mechanics. If you are having electrical signal problems, see ValJean."

In the picture of ValJean, he was standing next to a table, holding what appeared to be a soldering iron and leaning over a model airplane. The model looked like a P51 Mustang.

CHAPTER THIRTY EIGHT

I told Spencer Adams about the call from Richard in hopes that he might have an idea on how to track down the model airplane manufacturer to see if they had sold an extra receiver to ValJean Dupont. I told him about the faxes I had reviewed and showed him the picture of the model XM15. He agreed that it looked like a P51.

"Do you think that receiver could have been used to control the fuel shut off valve on an actual aircraft?"

"Sorry, Kip," he said. "I fly these airplanes, but I've never flown the model ones. My advice would be to look for clubs of enthusiasts who fly the models, ask someone in a club. Most of the people who fly models have had an interest in them from a young age, you may find someone who remembers that particular model."

"Good idea," I said, and thanked him.

We flew without much conversation, south and west towards the same area we had searched before, but lower. After we left the Miami flight pattern area, we were free to drop to a much lower altitude. Somewhere in this vast area of swamp grass and bays was a domed raft, I felt sure of that.

"Can we take it out over the coast line a little, Spence?" I asked.

"Sure," he said, and made a slow sweeping turn to the left, dropping another fifty or seventy five feet of altitude. I could see Buttonwood Canal going north from the coast line.

The steady hum of the Lycoming O-145 engine and the sound of the wind past the struts was all I could hear without the earphones. The overhead wing allowed excellent visibility below us. We flew maybe fifteen miles out over the bay.

"How far out do you want to go?" Spence asked.

"I guess this is far enough," I said. "He wouldn't risk taking the raft into open waters."

We made a right hand sweep past Buttonwood before heading north. I could see the canal on my right, like a small greenish blue ribbon, dangling from a darker green medallion at the top that was Coot's

Bay. I remembered the first time we searched this area and the recollection of a glimmer that might have been a solar panel on the dome raft.

We were still making a gradual sweeping turn and as we passed Coot's Bay I saw the same glimmer. It was like the reflection off of a window.

"What's that down there?" I pointed to the right and down .

"Don't know," Spence said. "I'll take her down and we'll have a look."

He tilted the airplane's nose down a bit and the right wing dipped, putting us in a slow spiraling turn with a radius of two or three miles. As we got lower, I could see the reflection clearer. At about 300 feet I saw that it was the dome raft!

"There he is," I said, pointing straight down.

"I see it," Spence said. "Nearest place to land is on Sugarloaf Key. You'd have to boat back to here. I think if we want to talk to ValJean we should fly back to the airport and drive down. It will be a lost faster than boating from Sugarloaf."

"We'd have to drive to Flamingo and rent a boat," I said.

"Yes, but it will still be faster than landing at Sugarloaf and boating back from there. We can be back at the airport in a half an hour. I'll let the airport crew put the airplane away and secure it, we can take your car or my truck and be in Flamingo in an hour and a half."

"That's two hours, would it take that long to boat up from Sugarloaf?"

"Maybe not, but we'd have to boat back to get the plane, then fly it home anyway. I'm in favor of flying home first, then driving down."

"OK," I said. "Let's do it."

CHAPTER THIRTY NINE

Forty five minutes later we were in Spencer's pickup truck headed back towards Coot's Bay. We stopped at the same rental place where I had rented the airboat to go fishing, and soon we were skimming across the swamps, headed in the general direction where we had seen the domed raft.

It was impossible to talk over the roar of the engine and the noise of the five foot props that propelled the airboat, so we communicated by hand signals when we thought we were getting off course, but we were headed in a generally west direction and I knew that eventually we would hit Buttonwood Canal and we could follow it north to Coot's Bay, then either follow the right hand curvature or head straight across.

When we got to Buttonwood, Spence slowed the airboat and made a gentle sweeping turn to the right, headed north. Almost immediately we were on Coot's Bay. He motioned to me with a right hand sweep and then a shrug with his shoulders, then a forward motion of his hand another shrug. I signaled back with a forward motion and we headed straight across the slightly deeper water of Coot's Bay, toward the northern edge where we had seen the raft.

Moments later it was in sight, and in less than two minutes Spence slowed the airboat, waited a few seconds then cut the engine to idle and I stepped forward with a line to tie up to the strange domed raft. As soon as I stepped on the raft I sensed that something was wrong. There was a feeling, an eerie, creepy tingling of the skin.

Spencer Adams must have felt it too.

"Be careful," he said.

I looped the line around a cleat on the raft and straightened up. I had started wearing my 9MM in a clamshell type holster, looped on my belt in the small of my back. I reached my arm around my back and got the gun.

I pointed the barrel to the sky, took my left hand and slid the action back and released it with an audible click, but left the safety in the "on" position. I was watching the hatch that led inside the raft.

"ValJean!" I yelled.

No answer.

I yelled again, raising the octave and volume of my voice, "ValJean!"

Still no answer.

The props on the airboat gave a final "*whuff, whuff,*" sound and then there was complete silence, not even the call of wild birds or the soothing sound of water lapping at the edges of the raft.

I took two steps toward the hatch before the smell reached my senses.

"God!" I said, involuntarily, and put my left hand over my nose and mouth.

"Hold on, Kip," Spence said. He boarded the raft and stepped up behind me, putting a hand on my shoulder.

"If that's what I think it is, we're too late to talk to ValJean."

I knew deep inside that what he was saying was true. I didn't want to believe it, but I sensed it when I first stepped on the raft, and the smell of death hung like a cloud around the dome. Someone was dead inside the raft.

I took two more careful steps and pulled the canvas curtain of the doorway aside. I could see feet and legs just inside the room, a dark stain under them.

Then I heard someone speak.

"Rudyard Kipling Yardley," a weak voice said.

My eyes shot to my left and across the room. ValJean sat on the edge of the bed, a shotgun cradled across his arm, pointing to his left.

I dropped my eyes to the body on the floor, then raised them quickly back to ValJean.

"What happened here?" I asked.

"They found me," he said, his voice a whisper.

I took a quick look behind me to see if Spencer Adams was there. He could be a witness to whatever it was I was about to find out.

"Who is they? And who's the corpse?"

"The big boys."

"What big boys, ValJean? Do you know who this corpse is? Did you shoot him?"

"I'm shot," he said, weakly.

I crossed the small space between us and took the shotgun from his hands.

I helped him lay down on the bed. A bloodstained piece of cloth fell from the left side of his chest, near his shoulder joint. There was a dark hole, surrounded by a purple ring, an inch to the right of his arm and an inch or so under his collar bone. The bullet had probably passed through without hitting bone, but it had caused a lot of damage to muscle.

"Don't suppose you've brought any thing to drink?"

"No," I said. "We've got to get you to a doctor, ValJean." I turned towards the door and saw that Spencer had entered the room and was headed towards us.

"I've got a friend with me, Spencer Adams," I said.

"Help me get him on the airboat," Spence said. "It's quicker to get him to a hospital if we take him than to call for paramedics."

"Agreed," I said.

"There's a tape recorder on the table," ValJean said. "Take the tape out and take it with you. If I don't make it, you'll know what happened here."

We lifted ValJean, me with my arms under his arms, and Spence with his arms around ValJean's plastic leg and good leg.

We got him on the airboat and took a few seconds to try to make him as comfortable as possible. I took off my tee-shirt and used it as a compress to place over the gunshot wound. Then I went back in the cabin and took the tape from the recorder and stuck it in my pocket.

I thought about trying to identify the dead man but the stench was so bad I had to get out of the cabin.

Spence had the motor started and as soon as I untied the airboat from the raft, he put the props in gear and we edged away, made a left turn towards the south and Spence gunned the engine. The props roared to a high pitch and we were soon skipping across Coot's Bay, headed back to the spot where we had left Spence's truck.

CHAPTER FORTY

I sat in Happs' office listening to the tape. Detective Happs listened intently to the voice of ValJean Dupont. At times the voice got so weak we had to lean forward and strain our ears to get it.

"Two men….. I heard the boat and felt it bump against my raft…..figured they'd come. I waited until they were both in the cabin….. The shotgun was under my kitchen table rigged and pointed at the door…. I pulled the cord ….the shotgun got one of them in the chest. The other one shot me……left on their boat. He's wounded, I don't know how bad. I won't make it….this tape may survive…. They are hit men from New York."

I thought about the day I had sat at that table and shared a drink with ValJean Dupont, and shuttered at the thought of what would have happened if he had accidentally tripped the cord that day.

"What do you think they were after?" I asked Happs.

"Don't know," he said. "We'll have to wait for ValJean to be well enough to talk, I guess. Doctors said it will be a day or so before we can talk to him."

Adams and I had rushed ValJean to the nearest hospital and I had put a call through to Happs. He had sent deputies to the dome raft and brought back the body. ValJean had lost a lot of blood and was nearly dead when Adams and I had arrived on the scene.

"Any ID on the corpse?" I asked.

"Nothing," he said. "Typical of a hit man. When a hit man goes out for the kill he leaves any identifying papers behind. We'll run a fingerprint ID through FBI records. If we're lucky we'll get a match. If the man didn't have a record, we may never know who he was."

"I wonder how ValJean knew they were hit men?"

"You looked for him for days," he said. "Obviously he was hiding out from something. Maybe he got word that someone had put a contract out on him."

"That's possible," I said. "What is it that ValJean did or what is it that he knows? Could it be that he has the goods on whoever killed Harry Fawn? Or does he know who killed Mona?"

"From what you've told me about the fuel shut off valve being rigged, I'd say it could be both," Happs said.

"We'll have some answers soon," I said. "I want to be there when you talk to him, if that's OK with you."

"If you'll promise you won't go blasting away at anyone who looks like they might be a hit man."

"You know me better than that."

"I don't know you at all, Yardley," he stopped the tape recorder, extracted the tape and put it in his desk drawer. "Sometimes I think you are a crack detective, and at other times I think you let your emotions get in the way of doing a good job."

"What's that supposed to mean?" I asked.

"If you had told me all you had found out about ValJean, his involvement with the airplane crash that killed Harry Fawn, his employment with the computer company that handled the lotto, I might have had someone watching him. Then he wouldn't be laying up there in that hospital, near death."

"That's bull crap and you know it. First of all, I did what any good police department *should* have done. I went looking for some answers and I found a few. I don't have all the pieces figured out, but I think ValJean knows more about it and that's why I was looking for him."

"Someone got to him before you did, Yardley."

"And the reason for that is something that I have yet to figure out. I've told you all I know about this case. If you haven't followed up on it, that's your problem. You seemed too busy warning me to stay away from Sarcosi."

"That's for your own good, Pal." He stood up and walked around his desk. "Let's not get at each other's throats, Yardley. I'm sorry if I upset you."

He stuck his hand out and I shook it.

"OK." I said. "Let me know when ValJean is ready to talk. Deal?"

"You got it."

CHAPTER FORTY ONE

I had a feeling I knew who had tipped the contract boys off. A private detective who might be burning the candle at both ends.

I knocked on the door of Stan Morgan's house and waited. No answer. I knocked again and waited another two minutes, still no-one appeared at the door. Just as I started to leave I heard the knob turning.

The door opened slowly and a Cuban woman stood looking at me. She gave me a quick once over and glanced over my shoulder to see if there were INS agents behind me.

"What you want?"

"I'm looking for Stan Morgan," I said.

"No live here, move."

"Where to?"

"Yo no se."

"¿Quiénes son los dueños de esta casa?" Who are the owners of this house?

"A través de la calle" Across the street.

"Gracias, Senora."

I walked back to the sidewalk and looked across the street to another house, nearly the duplicate of this one, except in a better state of repair. No harm trying, I thought and crossed the narrow street and knocked at the door of the house there.

The door opened immediately as if someone had been watching me.

"Can you tell me how to find Mr. Stan Morgan?" I asked the man who answered the door.

"No, I can't tell you exactly, Sir. He told me he was moving to Las Vegas."

"Vegas?"

"Yes. He asked me a few days ago if he could get out of his lease by paying me off. I told him that I would void the lease for two thousand dollars. That seemed to please him so he gave me the money in cash and I gave him back the lease."

"I don't suppose he left a forwarding address with the Postal Service either?" It wasn't a question, just a notion on my part.

"You'd have to ask the mailman, I suppose," the man told me.

"Well, thank you. I'll check with the post office. Can you tell me where the nearest post office is for this area?"

"Two streets over," he motioned behind him. "then two blocks down on the far side of the street."

"Thanks."

I got in the Lincoln and drove to the post office. They hesitated to give me any information at all citing homeland security regulations.

Back in the car I called Happs and asked him if there was anything he could do to get an address for Morgan. He promised to check and call me back.

Then I called Toby Smith.

He berated me for not keeping him posted on what I was doing in Florida, asked when I'd be coming back to LA and told me again that the CHP was not my own private information service, but finally agreed to put out some feelers on Stan Morgan in Las Vegas.

I thanked him and hung up the phone.

A car went by slowly on my left.

I don't even bother to explain to friends and relatives how I know when something is wrong. Call it intuition, call in instinct, call it many years of living on the edge of danger brought about by association with hoods and criminals and hard cases of all kinds. The low life in LA.

Call it what you want. I don't care. What I care about is this: It saved my life.

I was already ducking below the level of the glass in the passenger side window when the shotgun went off. Glass spewed all over me. I grabbed the 9MM from the holster in the small of my back, opened the car door and dove for the pavement. I hit and rolled hard three times, saw the car speeding away down the street. I raised the gun and fired three rounds from the prone position, at the back window of the car. One slug hit the trunk, I have no idea where the other two went. The car was too far away.

I scrambled to my feet and literally jumped back in the Lincoln, twisted the key hard and as soon as the engine caught, pulled the gear shift lever down hard to "L" and stomped the accelerator. The big car screamed away, leaving a trail of melted rubber on the pavement. At the corner ahead I saw the car run right. I kept my right foot jammed on the gas feed and made the same right turn on two wheels, the big eight cylinder engine screaming.

As I went around the corner, the car ahead was turning left at the next street. I realized that with that much of a lead my chances of catching it were slim and none. The driver of the getaway car knew the area, I didn't. My heart was beating so hard in my chest I thought I could hear it.

If those were Sarcosi's hoods, I'd had enough. A two second delay in ducking my head and I'd be missing the left side of my face.

I drove straight to Happs' office and filed a report.

"That's what I've been trying to tell you, Yardley," he told me. "Sarcosi is not just a minor player with the mob. He's got connections that go back a long way. If he wants you dead, he'll eventually succeed."

"Yeah, you told me already," I said. "I'm not sure that was Sarcosi's hoods. Maybe there's somebody else who would like me dead."

"Who?" he said, deadpan.

"How the hell should I know," I said. "I have a feeling I'm getting close to whoever killed Mona, and maybe closer to flushing out the missing lotto ticket. Whoever took a shot at me might be the same guy that ValJean chased off of his raft."

"Speaking of ValJean," Happs said, "I just got a call from the hospital. He's stable and able to talk to us. I can't go until later this evening. If you want to go, go ahead."

"I have to report the window incident to the car rental place, then I'll go."

"OK" he said.

CHAPTER FORTY TWO

ValJean Dupont looked a whole lot better sitting up in his hospital bed than he did setting on the edge of his bunk where I'd found him, half dead.

"Glad to see you're still in the land of the living, ValJean," I said, smiling.

"Rudyard Kipling Yardley," he said, grinning back at me.

"I've listened to your tape," I told him. "What more can you tell me about this entire scenario. I know you're the one who put the radio control valve on Harry Fawn's airplane. I don't know who paid you to do it, but I'm convinced you're the mechanic that put it on there."

"Do you want me to confess now, or later, after Detective Happs gets here?"

"Whatever you tell me will be between the two of us," I said. "Happs has his own way of investigating, I have mine. Besides, I've got an axe to grind now. Somebody just tried to take my head off with a shotgun."

"You?"

"Yeah, me." I said. "Does that surprise you?"

"I guess it does," he said. "See, I'm not really talking to you. I'm dead."

"Dead?"

"Yeah. Happs called me and asked me if I would object to him putting out the word that I was found dead on my raft. It made the papers this morning, look at this."

He handed me a Miami newspaper. Front page picture was of his domed raft. Headlines read:

"Homestead Man Found Dead on Raft."

I read the first three paragraphs. It described how Homestead detectives had been alerted that there was a body on board a raft in Coot's Bay. When they arrived they found the body of Homestead legendary veteran, ValJean Dupont.

ValJean had no known relatives in the area, according to the paper, and police had waited two days before announcing his demise.

I looked up at ValJean.

"What's the reason for this?" I asked.

"I don't know what Happs has in mind," he said.

"So what does the doctor say about your wound?"

"He says I'll live," ValJean said. "Little does he know."

"Let's get back to the question on the table, ValJean," I said. "Did you put that valve on Harry Fawn's airplane?"

"No." He said. That surprised me. I'd figured him for that.

"No? I found where you bought the radio controlled plane that had the device used to control that valve."

"I did that," he said, looking away. His eyes became a little cloudy.

"But you didn't put it on the plane?"

"I told you I didn't. I built the damned thing, but I had nothing to do with it after that. I didn't know what they planned on doing with it."

"Who are *they*?"

"The guys who paid me to build it," he said.

"Tell me about it, ValJean," I said. "Let's don't play patty cake with each other."

"I was just out of high school then," he said. "I'd not found a good job, just making pizza in a deli. You know the place. Alfredo's."

"Sarcosi?"

"That's the one. I had talked to employees there about my hobby of flying model airplanes. I even showed them some magazines with pictures of my planes. One day Al Sarcosi asked me if I could put a radio controlled device on a regular aircraft part. I said I could if I had access to machines to make the modification. He brought me the valve and gave me money to rent a machine at a local machine shop. I bought the RC device and made an adapter. It wasn't hard to do."

"Did you realize that it was your valve that brought down Harry Fawn's airplane?"

"Not at the time," he said. "By the time they used it, I had joined the Army. I pulled a tour of duty overseas. When I came back I heard about Fawn's plane. I had a relationship with Mona before the Army, and it worried me that Sarcosi might have put that valve on Harry's plane."

"Speaking of Mona," I interrupted, "Do you know why she couldn't read?"

"No, but I have a valid suspicion."

"Why?"

"Because of a letter I wrote to her. After I did some investigating and bought the parts of her father's wrecked aircraft, I knew it was my RC valve that brought it down. I wrote Mona a letter and told her that I couldn't see her any more. I couldn't face her personally at that time, so I wrote the letter."

"In the letter I told her about making the valve for Sarcosi. I warned her not to mention it to anyone, ever. I told her that if Sarcosi knew that she knew about that valve, her life might be in danger. As it turned out, I was right."

"Do you think Sarcosi killed her because she knew about the valve?"

"I'm sure of it," he said. "I can't prove it, but I'm convinced it was Sarcosi's kid that killed her."

"How did Sarcosi know that she knew?"

"I told him."

"What?"

"How much pain do you think a man can take, Kip Yardley?" he asked me.

I remained silent. He continued.

"At first the blade of the chain saw felt like a scratch, then immediately a burning flame of pain erupted across my thigh. I jerked as hard as I could, a natural reflex action, away from the source of pain. It was a futile reaction."

"The blade inched it's way slowly into the nerves below the skin, the flame of pain became intense, a heat that seared into my mind. I screamed. They knew what they were doing. It wasn't quick, get it over with, it was micrometer at a time, like carving a delicate ice sculpture with a chain saw."

"That's how you lost your leg?"

He shook his head. "I screamed and begged. My throat was raw from screaming. Have you ever experienced that kind of relentless pain, Kip?"

I sat there transfixed, listening.

"When the ripping teeth of the chain saw blade crept into the muscle of my leg it was unbearable. I fainted. And so it went, pain, fainting, awakening, pain. I was out of my mind with pain. Demons with pitchforks were attacking my leg. Incessant, cruel, grinding, torturous pain invaded the delicate membranes of my brain. My cells were being attacked, I pictured alligators chewing on my leg."

"They knew what they were doing all right. They knew I would keep their deadly secret. And I kept it. Now I don't care anymore. I'll tell you what you want to know. They can't hurt me now. The whiskey has killed me. My liver is fried. My brain is cooked from the pain. The only woman I ever loved is gone. Dead. They thought they had me hooked forever. I'm going to be free now. It will all be over in a matter of minutes. No more pain, no more memories. Happs didn't know he was predicting my real death."

"What are you talking about?" I asked, suddenly keenly aware of his last few words.

"I'm talking about morphine," ValJean said. "I got up early this morning, Kip. Before anyone else, I suppose. I borrowed some tools from the nurse's desk, a pair of scissors and a nail file. I got into the cabinet where the drugs are kept."

He lifted his left arm and in his hand I saw the needle connected to the IV drip tube.

"I was a medic in the service," he said. "You probably know that much about me. This stuff will soon be pounding through my veins, and I'll get sleepy. In four minutes I'll be sound asleep. In about six minutes my heart will simply stop beating."

"I'm not going to let you do that, ValJean." I said.

"You'll stop me?" he asked.

"Yes."

"I'm asking you not to," he said. A certain sadness appeared in his eyes.

"You're one of the last of the good guys. Don't interfere with this, Kip. I'm begging you. They got to me and if I live they'll find me again, sooner or later, and when they do, they'll cut off my other leg with a chain saw, like they did this one." He lifted his stump of a leg and slid it out from under the thin hospital sheet.

"Why do they want you now?" I asked.

"It isn't me they want. It's the ticket. They want to make sure it doesn't get cashed."

"You have the ticket?" I asked, immediately my mind started thinking of the possibilities.

"I know where it is. See, Kip, I fixed it so Mona would win."

"You fixed it?"

"Yes. Mona always played the same numbers. All I had to do was program the computer to make sure those numbers appeared. I did it all the time. Whatever numbers they wanted to win they fed me. I hacked into the computer and fed it her numbers. The numbers won."

"You controlled the outcome?"

"Yes. But the secret isn't in who wins. The secret is programming the computer so no-one wins."

"You can do that?"

"It's just as easy. After the lotto closes, the computer knows every number that was played, so I simply programmed the computer to search the list, print a number that did *NOT* appear on the list. I just modified Harry Fawn's program a little."

"And the reason for that?"

"The pot grows. When the pot is big enough someone in the mob wins, burns the ticket, and the winnings are never dispersed."

"I'm beginning to see some light here, ValJean. But what makes you want to give up? You've got the answer to the whole puzzle. When Happs gets here, just tell him what you've told me. That will put the bad guys in the clink and you can relax. No need to go to sleep with morphine dreams."

"That won't stop the suffering, Kip." He said, his eyes misting again. "Besides I'm already dead. Remember?"

"What suffering? I realize now what you went through, and Mona's loss is a loss to all of us, particularly Tami. I'm sure you are strong enough to get over that, ValJean, if you got over the loss of your leg, you can get over Mona's death."

"But not the guilt," he said. "And the suffering isn't all mental. You see, Kip, I've been suffering from liver cancer for quite some time. The pain gets consecutively worse. Morphine is an easy way out. I'll just go to sleep."

"I can't let you do that, ValJean." I said.

"You'd let me suffer? You know I can't stand the pain. I'll go crazy if I have to live with pain until I die. Even if I live, I might still wind up losing my other leg to the mob. Why not let me go out my way? I'd do the same for you."

"I've got more to learn from you," I said.

"Ask."

"For starters, why did they wait until now to kill Mona? If you told them that she knew about the valve when you lost your leg, why didn't they go after her then?"

"They knew she wouldn't say anything. They told her if she talked, her husband and Tami would lose their legs like I did. Besides, she still loved me."

"When did you get the ticket? And where is it now?"

"Mona brought it to me on the beach."

I asked the question I had to ask:

"Who killed Mona Fawn?"

"I don't know. If I had to guess I'd say it was young Sarcosi. He's the craziest of the two. It's a long, sad story, Kip Yardley."

"Tell me," I said.

"I made the biggest mistake of my life when I agreed to make the fuel shut off valve for that airplane," he said. "They didn't tell me who's plane it was and I didn't ask. They offered me ten grand to do it. I needed the money. Then when I found out it was Harry Fawn's airplane it killed me.. he was Mona's father, and when I told Mona that I was the one who killed her Dad, it was all over for us. As it turned out, it was all over anyway. I got the word that I was never to see Mona again, that I was never to let anyone know the truth. You see, Kip Yardley, I am Tami's father."

"Your Tami's father? I figured as much." I said. "What about the night Mona was killed?"

"The local boys wanted me rig the computer to print the winning ticket, one that would never be cashed. I fixed it, OK. I fixed it so Mona's numbers would win.

"As soon as the winning numbers were announced I got a call. The mafia knew that I had betrayed them. They told me to get the ticket and deliver it to Sarcosi."

"I called her the night she won. She told me you and Tami had gone for some wine. We agreed to meet in the cove near where she was found after Tami was asleep. When I got there she was already there. We talked. I asked her for the ticket and she gave it to me. The Sarcosi kid and that other idiot were waiting nearby, I was supposed to give it to them. Then the Sarcosi kid came charging through the saw grass. I had just enough time to hide the ticket. I put it under a rock on the beach."

"He told Mona to give him the ticket and she said she didn't have it. He called her a lying bitch, and a bunch of other things. I took a swing at him and he knocked me on my ass. The next thing I knew I woke up and it was daylight. I saw Mona's body laying there. I got the ticket from under the rock and went back to where I'd left my truck. All four tires were flat. I walked to the convenience store and got a cab home. It was when I went back for my truck that I met you. I didn't have the cash to pay the guy who fixed the flats."

"I was supposed to give the ticket to Sarcosi. They had someone waiting in the background who would actually claim the money. Of course the mob would be the ones who GOT the money. They might pay the stooge who cashed it a pittance, but more than a hundred million? Not in a million years."

"Do you know who that someone was?"

"Just a guess, Kip." He took a long breath. "I think the guy who was ultimately going to cash the ticket was a lawyer named Gene."

"If they didn't cash it, the school board would get the biggest chunk of the money. William Stevens would then siphon it off to complete a real estate project controlled by the mob."

That explained how Stevens fit into the picture.

"So I was damned if I did and damned if I didn't," he said. "The Mafia was going to win. Either the local mob or the New York mob. The locals if the ticket is cashed, the New Yorkers if it is not cashed. And to think that the only person in my life who ever cared for me had to die because of my stupidity."

He sobbed loudly twice, pushed the plunger and immediately I could see him relax.

"Where's the ticket, ValJean?"

His eyes rolled up and back and he said slowly,

"You almost bought it from me for forty bucks."

Then his eyes fluttered a few times and he went to sleep.

CHAPTER FORTY THREE

I didn't wait for Happs to get there. I had other things to do. I called Toby Smith in California. He had found an address for Morgan in Las Vegas. A midnight special out of Miami had a seat in first class and I took it. The flight was uneventful except for my thoughts. My brain was rattling like dice.

I needed to know who Morgan had talked to. Sometimes false leads will spring up in a case and investigators will spend days barking up the wrong tree. I wanted to avoid that if possible so I figured if Morgan wouldn't talk I'd beat it out of him. My patience was wearing thin.

A good friend had been killed. Another friend had been duped into a conspiracy that cost him a leg, a liver, then his life. A shotgun had almost taken my own life. I'd had to play hardball a time or two in my career, and now was a time when I wasn't adverse to being a little on the cold blooded side.

I found Morgan at a cheap hotel. He was alone and surprised to see me.

"What do you want with me, Yardley?"

"I want to know who you sold out to, Morgan. I know you were working for Charles DuPont, but who did you sell the information to, DuPont or the New York mob?"

"I don't know what you're talking about," he said.

That's when I hit him.

He hit the floor on his spreading behind and then his head hit. I dropped to the floor with a knee on each side of his chest and got a left hand full of his hair, raised his head and popped it hard on the floor again.

"Give me a name, Morgan, or so help me I'm going to crack your skull like a watermelon."

"Your nuts, Yardley," he screamed. "Get off of me, leave me alone!"

"Talk to me, Morgan," I said, and popped his head again.

"GG..."

"What?"

"George Geoncelli," he said. "He gave me ten grand."

"What did you give him?"

"I gave him that boat freak, ValJean DuPont."

"How'd you find ValJean?" I asked, curious.

"I followed you," he said.

"No way. By the time I found ValJean the mob boys had already been there!"

"I followed you the first time," he said. "I tagged you to the geodesic dome convention; I asked questions from the same people you asked. When you talked to the pilot guy I was listening on a special phone with a frequency finder. I'm a licensed pilot so I got ahead of you to the airport and rented a plane. I was behind you all day."

"I didn't find ValJean that day," I said.

"You missed your chance then," he said, "Now will you let me up?"

"Talk to me some more," I said.

"I saw light reflecting off of something in Coot's Bay," he said. "You either didn't see it or it didn't dawn on you that it might be a solar panel from that one legged weirdo's boat. He's a real nut case."

I thought about that day and remembered seeing something glitter far below us....*it was the geodesic dome raft that I had seen.*

I lost it then. I raised his head and bonked it again. ValJean was definitely not a nut case. He was, in all reality, a genius. A master of many things. It irritated me to hear someone call him a nut case less than 24 hours after I watched him pump his veins full of morphine and go to sleep, never to feel pain again.

"Damn you, Yardley," Morgan squealed. "I'm talking, why are you still cracking my skull?"

"Because I feel like it," I said.

I got up slowly and yanked on Morgan's tie. His chest came up fast for a big man. His head hit me in the gut and knocked me backwards. I stumbled and by the time I reacted he was on his feet, big arms reaching for me.

I did a double inside block, both fists at chest level, arms swept upward then out, knocking both of his arms away from his sides. Then I brought both hands knife edge down on the sides of his neck. He went out like a light.

I had the information I needed. I took a lamp cord and tied his wrists together with his hands behind him, tied his ankles together and finished by using the TV cord to tie his wrists and ankles to the bed leg. That way he couldn't get to the phone and have the cops looking for me.

I had taken a cab from the airport to the hotel and called another one from the lobby to take me back. There was a flight for Jacksonville leaving in an hour so I bought a ticket and had a beer and burritos in a Mexican joint. Four hours later I was back in Florida.

It was after midnight and I was feeling my age. I took a cab to a motel near the airport and slept for six hours. After a long shower and breakfast I took another cab to the rental place where I had left my Austin Healey, and minutes later I was on 95 headed for Miami. It felt great to be behind the wheel of the Healey once more.

CHAPTER FORTY FOUR

I called Toby Smith and asked for a rundown on George Geoncelli. He called me back twenty minutes later with some disturbing details. Geoncelli was a hit man for the New York mob. He had served some time at Attica for assault with a deadly weapon. A contract that he had went sour and the man didn't die. He fingered Geoncelli but had no real proof. The court discerned that Geoncelli had indeed assaulted the man, but couldn't prove intent to kill.

He had been seen in LA during the past week. Hospital records indicated he had been treated for what appeared to be gunshot wounds, Geoncelli said he'd been hunting with a friend and the friend had accidentally shot him with a shotgun. No charges were pressed against the friend, and police investigation failed to locate the shooter. There were no witnesses.

It was plain to me that George Geoncelli, known in the underworld as GG or GiGi, was one of the hoods who had attacked ValJean DuPont. Toby had done his homework and found that GiGi had checked out of the hospital, out of his motel, and purchased a one way ticket to Miami. I had an idea that GiGi was one of the hoods who had attacked me at the parking lot of the mall. I remembered the diamond ring with the letters G.G. on it.   If I was right, he worked for Alberto Sarcosi.

I thanked Toby, in my politest manner I told him to send a bill to the firm's address in Santa Monica, and hung up.

I thought about calling Happs and asking him to pick up George Geoncelli for questioning.   Then I realized that GiGi wasn't going to open up to any line of questioning, that his alibi would be airtight, and that Happs would be wasting his time. Then I thought about calling the former Green County Tennessee sheriff, Spencer Adams, for some backup. Then I thought of calling the Florida State Police, then the FBI, then the Secret Service and my convoluted, confused brain decided that even the U.S. Army wasn't going to help me. This was something I had to do by myself, and if it got me killed, then that was just the way of the world.

I drove to Sarcosi's deli, parked the Austin Healey as far away from the door to the deli as I dared, thinking I might have to make a run for it. I didn't go in right away, but watched the door. A concrete wall hid the Healey from passersby along the entrance to the strip mall.

I was parked under a fan palm and there was a cool breeze blowing that I was thankful for. I sat there watching the door, at times letting my mind drift a little. I wanted to see Tami. I wanted to hold her close to me and tell her that everything was going to be OK. I hadn't seen her in nearly a week, and the ache in my soul was spreading. I realized that sooner or later I would have to ask her. That realization scared me. If she wanted a permanent relation with me, as Rhonda did, then I had to do some soul searching.

My subconscious saw a beautifully restored 1984 Cadillac Eldorado convertible drive through the lot. There were two men in it. One was Sarcosi, in the passenger seat, the other was the big, crew cut wearing guy who wore a diamond ring with the initials G.G.

I tensed all over, then forced myself to relax. I felt for my gun, pulled it out and checked the clip, slid the barrel back and let it snap, then set the safety. The two men were getting out of the car and walking towards the door of the deli.

I didn't know what my plan of action was going to be, only that I needed some answers.

I waited until the two men went inside, then walked to the car. It was easy to reach over the door and pull the hood release. I raised the hood, pulled the distributor wire loose from the coil and closed the hood. I started for the door of the deli and then veered away from it. My reason for disabling the Cadillac was to keep GiGi from running, but I realized that a better plan was hatching in my head.

I walked into a souvenir shop next to the deli, browsed around until the manager started getting nervous, bought a book about seashells, and left. On the other side of the deli was a fast food Chinese place. I went in and stood in line until it came my turn to order, got a couple of egg rolls and a coke with lots of ice. sat by the window, watching the Cadillac.

Half way through the second egg roll I saw GiGi leave the deli and head to his car.

He got in and cranked the engine a few times. From where I sat I could see a puzzled look cross his broad face. I got up and stood near the door for a minute pretending to look for my keys.

GiGi got out of the car and went to the front of it, raised the hood and stood looking under it. I opened the door and walked quietly and quickly up behind him. When he bent at the waist and put his head and shoulders under the hood, I grabbed the hood and slammed it as hard as my 178 pounds would let me. I heard the "thonk" as it hit his head and he went limp. I raised the hood and GiGi slid down the front of the big car into a dazed lump.

I put my 9MM in my right hand and dumped the remainder of my coke and ice on his head. He shook his head and looked up at me.

"Carlos send you?" He said, grimacing.

"Get up, GiGi," I said. "We're going for a ride."

"I'll break your frickin' neck," he said.

I stood far enough away from him to prevent any sudden movements to overpower me.

"Get up," I repeated.

He grabbed the front bumper of the car and hauled himself to his knees, put one foot under himself and stood up.

"Get in," I said. "You drive."

As he walked to the drivers side of the car I pushed the ignition wire back in the coil and closed the hood. I had the gun pointed at him all the time and let myself into the passenger seat.

"Drive," I said.

He started the car and put it in gear.

"Which way?" he asked, shaking his head. I could see a streak of blood oozing down the side of his head, around his ear, and down his neck, before running under the collar of the $100 shirt he wore.

"Turn left out of the lot," I said, and he obliged. I directed him to drive away from Homestead, down the highway towards the Everglade swamps, to the outskirts of town. A lot of information was trickling through my mind. Some of it was starting to make sense, some I still had to play by ear. One of those bits of information was Carlos Fawn's connection with the Mafia.

I directed GiGi to Carlos Fawn's house. When we got there I ordered him out of the car and up to the door.

"Ring the bell," I ordered.

He rang it.

Carlos came to the door, opened it and looked at GiGi.

"Yes?" Carlos said.

I stepped from behind GiGi and motioned at the crew cut wearing hood.

"Know this guy, Carlos?"

Carlos looked at me with a slight frown on his face. It was like I was the last person in the world he expected to show up with GiGi in tow.

"Yeah, he looks familiar," Carlos said. "I think he's a New York Mafioso."

"Can we come in?" I asked.

Carlos stood aside and we went in. Carlos closed the door behind him as we entered.

"I need to make him answer some questions, Carlos," I said. "I have information that he's a hit man, and the one who is responsible for the death of ValJean DuPont."

"You're nuts!" GiGi said.

"Maybe," I said. "I tracked down a friend of yours, a PI named Morgan. He tells me that he gave you the place DuPont had his boat, and you gave him ten grand in cash. Does that sound familiar?"

"Go to hell!" he said.

"So what do you want from me?" Carlos asked.

"You want to find out who killed your son. Maybe you have a way of convincing him to talk?" I said.

"There's a million ways that have been used to make men talk," he said. "I know of one that has always been effective."

"Do it," I told him.

"I'll need your help," he said. "And we'll have to take him somewhere else, we can't do it here."

"Let's do it," I said.

"Just a minute," he said and took a ring of keys from his pocket.

He went out the back door and I nudged GiGi to move to a window so I could watch what Carlos was doing. He went to an outside building, a small 8 x 12 storage shed, unlocked the door and went in. When he came out he was carrying a chain saw.

CHAPTER FORTY FIVE

The Everglades have many miles of "tunnels", mangrove trees that have grown together near the top, forming tunnels above canals from one pond to another, Some of the tunnels are more than a mile long, alligators line the banks. Some of the mangrove trees have formed the arch of the tunnel so low to the water that they are impassable.

Here and there through the swamps the National Parks Service has built platforms on the banks of the canals so that people can camp in relative safety from the alligators.

It was at one of these platforms that Carlos directed me to tie up the airboat that we had rented near his house.

Our prisoner, George Geoncelli, or GiGi, had remained quiet. Now he was acting nervous and glancing first at me, then at Carlos. Occasionally his eyes drifted to the chainsaw that Carlos was carrying.

"Tie him to the pylons," Carlos said.

I took a length of rope from the deck of the airboat and tied GiGi securely to the pylon posts of the deck.

"You ask the questions," Carlos told me. "If he won't talk, I'll persuade him."

I turned my back on Carlos and faced GiGi.

"First, I want to know who the top dog is in this. Who gave you orders to kill ValJean Dupont?"

GiGi looked at me, his eyes starting to show a glimpse of fear. He looked at the chain saw again, and back at me.

"You stupid shit," he said, his mouth twisting in a dark grimace. "Don't you know you asked the wrong man to help you make me talk?"

His eyes went behind me to Carlos.

I turned and looked into the eyes of a cruel killer.

"You," I said.

Carlos pointed a .38 at my chest and shook his head slowly back and forth.

"You just don't know when to quit, do you, Yardley?"

"Just what part did you play in this?" I asked.

"What you wanted to find out is who killed my son," he said. "I'll tell you. I killed him."

"You?"

"Yes, me. Oh I didn't do it intentionally or personally. I didn't know who the victim was going to be, I thought it was going to be Sarcosi."

"What the hell are you trying to tell me, Carlos? You killed your own son? You thought you were killing Sarcosi?"

"I paid for the valve they put the valve on my son's airplane," he said. "Sarcosi wanted to be the next Don Corleone. Harry was giving Sarcosi flying lessons at the time. When we got word that Sarcosi was siphoning money off the top and planning on giving me to the Feds, Harry thought of the airplane. No one would ever suspect he rigged his own plane, it was supposed to crash when Sarcosi took his solo flight."

His eyes got misty with tears. "He was my pride and joy. He always did exactly what I told him to do, and he was my choice to take my place.

"Your place?"

"Yeah, my place. You see Yardley, the mob has quite a few members who are always

trying to climb higher in the hierarchy. I'd
reached the peak. I was calling the shots here
in Miami. The New York boys were pleased
with my efforts. We had the complete real
estate market down here. Nothing got
bought, sold or built without money going
through our hands."

"It was the same with the Lotto. We
controlled it. Harry had the program down
pat. We could make the winner whoever we
wanted to be. By controlling the winning
tickets that were never claimed, we siphoned
off the cream."

"How'd you get the Lotto
Commissioner to go along with that?" I
asked.

"Ollie LaFluer?"

"Yeah, the fat man in Jacksonville," I
said.

"He's been on the payroll since we put
him there," he said. "He's just one of many
state lotto commissioners that work for the
Mafia."

"And you? Where do you fit?"

"I am Mafia," he said. "I started this
years ago. Nothing happened without the
Union. I controlled the union. Power begets
power, Yardley."

"Why did you disappear then," I asked. What caused you to go underground?"

"Sarcosi squealed." He said. "The feds knew who I was, Carlos Fawn. They had me. I decided it was best to give up my title of "Godfather" and stay out of the pen. Most of the money I had stashed away is still in place. I'm content to let my replacement run things. That way I stay out of jail and alive."

"So you killed your own son. The Mafia convinced you to kill your own son?"

"Are you that dense, Yardley?" he asked.

"I'm not following all of this very well," I admitted.

"Word got to me that the New York boys were going to blow Harry's plane out of the sky. We wanted to get Sarcosi on his solo flight but Harry's flight to New York was called suddenly. If we cancelled it, Sarcosi might get wise. I knew that Sarcosi was going to be the trigger man on the transmitter. I had ValJean DuPont rig another transmitter, just like the first one, but with explosives in it. Someone else must have got to him."

"As the airplane approached, Sarcosi pushed a button that was supposed to blow him to smithereens. Instead, it blew my poor son to hell. Along with him, it killed his wife, the mother of Mona."

"Why am I tied up?" GiGi asked suddenly. "I didn't have anything to do with that."

"You're as dumb as Yardley," Carlos said. "You got the hit contract for ValJean DuPont. You blew that deal. Then you were supposed to off Yardley and you blew that one. Now, I want to make sure you never talk."

"Let's get back to you, Carlos. You told me you didn't know who killed your son," I said. "You were anxious to find out. 'They'll be turning to caca in the belly of an alligator' is what you told me."

"Whoever clued Sarcosi in on the transmitter is the sinvergüenza cabron that killed my son," he said. "That is the name I've been wanting. That's what Cliff Stone was trying to give me."

All the time that Carlos spent talking I had spent thinking. I knew that he wasn't going to walk away and leave me alive. It figured that he was going to kill GiGi, make it look like I had done that job, then kill me and make my body disappear into the evil of the Everglades.

Nothing replaces fear.

I've faced the final curtain a few times and like Sinatra, I did it my way. That's why I am still living and a few really bad guys are not. But now I was as frightened as I'd ever been in my life. I knew that Carlos could shoot me long before I could get my hand behind my back and grab my own gun.

"Pick up the saw, Yardley. You're going to operate on our friend here."

I thought of a hundred things I could say, all of them flashed through my mind like watching the final few minutes of old television mysteries.

"You'll never get away with this,"

"What makes you think I'll cooperate?"

"You're nuts!"

"You'll have to kill me too."

All of the catch phrases that everyone from Mike Hammer to Magnum, P.I. had used over the years went slicing through my mind. Nothing fit.

I picked up the saw.

"Fire it up," Carlos said with a slight motion of his hand, the one holding the gun.

I've seen people start chain saws on the first pull. I held it in my left hand, grasped the rope firmly with my right and pulled. Nothing but a slight growl.

An idea started to crawl through the fear, growling in my head like the chain saw.

It wasn't much, but it was all I had. I locked the throttle wide open.

I pushed the saw away from me firmly and yanked with my right hand on the cord. It started. I whirled as fast as I could and swept the chainsaw out and up. In my minds eye it was traveling in slow motion, the blade rose slowly, the chain spinning, the sound echoing through my head.

"R-R-R-R-R-R-R-R-R-R" in slow motion, the pitch low and growling.

Carlos jumped back fast but not fast enough. The blade hit him in the chest. A wild shot boomed from his gun filling the air, blending with the growl of the saw. I saw the spurt of blood as I moved, but it still hit me. My left leg was covered with blood and for a split second I thought it was my own. Fear surged like icicles through my brain. I dropped the saw and jumped. The saw hit the wooden deck, blades still howling, slicing chunks out of the wooden planks.

My movement was quick and to my right.

Carlos screamed. His gun hand swept around towards me, arm stretched out in front of his body. Blood pumped in spurts from a gaping wound in his chest where the saw blade had sliced open his ribs. He pulled the trigger in some frenzied, maniacal effort to finish what he had started. It was too late. The slug missed me by two feet and then it was over.

Carlos lay dying on the deck. I needed more answers. It was now or never.

"You knew they were going to kill Harry and you rigged the transmitter to kill Sarcosi instead?"

He looked at me with wild eyes.

"Yes," he whispered, barely audible.

"Who's the New York Capo?"

"DuPont."

"ValJean DuPont was the head of the Big Apple mob?" I asked in disbelief.

"Charles," he said, sucking in his breath with a gurgling sound. "Charles is the Godfather."

"Charles DuPont?"

It was too late. Whatever other information Carlos had to tell me would have to be found elsewhere. Carlos was dead.

I left GiGi tied to the platform, took the airboat back to where I could pick up GiGi's car and drove back to Miami. I needed time to think. This case was getting to be a headache, too many twists, too many variables. I couldn't believe that Charles DuPont was the head of the New York Mafia. That would mean that he ordered the murder of his own daughter and his grand daughter, and then hired me to find their killers.

CHAPTER FORTY SIX

Carlesi DePonteri. It was right there in black and white. Head of the New York Mafia. Born in Italy, 1929. Immigrated to New York as a child in 1933. Served as an apprentice to the Cosa Nostra from 1945 to 1960, armed bodyguard for the Giancanas.

Moved up in the ranks circa 1962 upon the death of Joseph Profaci when Joseph Magliocco appeared to take control over the crime family leadership. Magliocco's girl friend was from Sicily and believed to be the sister of Carlesi DePonteri. Charles DuPont was never mentioned by name in the book.

My first stop after returning to Miami was at the police station where I told my story to Happs. He wanted me to take him back to the platform in the swamps where Carlos's body was laying next to the hoodlum, GiGi. I declined. I guess he could have forced me under some law or another, but either he wasn't in the mood for enforcing his request or knew that my time would be better spent elsewhere.

I drove back to the Deli parking lot, left GiGi's car and took the Healey to my motel room where I showered and changed. Next stop, the library.

So it was at the library where I sat pondering over the entire case. I had a tablet next to me, making notes, and a copy of the book by Emory Letchman, "History of the Cosa Nostra in America."

The first note that I made on the tablet was this:

"Is it possible that this is the reason for Mona's inability to read and write? Could she have read this and somehow connected Carlesi DePonteri to her grandfather, Charles Dupont?"

I continued reading the book, fascinated by the ups and downs of characters who were heads of Mafia families. Then I found the next one. Charlie Cervato started as a union organizer when the railroad crept into northern Florida. By the time it reached Homestead, Cervato had escalated in rank and power to a position where the railroad couldn't drive a spike unless he said it was OK. The book went on to describe how Cervato's influence spread into drugs, prostitution, gambling, real estate development, and politics.

By the early seventies Cervato had accumulated enough power and wealth to take over the Cosa Nostra in Florida. He was the kingpin, or as described by Letchman, "The Organizer." There was a hint as to how wide spread Cervato's influence fell in a paragraph ".....when the lotto came to Florida, the state politicians had to get permission from Cervato."

Strangely, Letchman had never made the connection between Carlos Fawn "a minor player in the mob" and Charlie Cervato. Neither had he connected "Carlesi DePonteri" with Charles DuPont. If he had made those connections he might not have lived to finish his book.

Now I was almost certain that this book was the primary cause of Mona's reading disability. She had understood what the book said. She knew that there was a possibility that her parents were killed by members of the Mafia and now she had uncovered evidence that the Mafia was controlled by her grandfathers. I made a note of that on my tablet.

The book went on to say that Joseph Valachi had blown the whistle on Florida Cosa Nostra. Top leaders began to fall like dominos. No names were mentioned, but it didn't take a rocket scientist to know that Charlie Cervato was one of the top leaders that disappeared. He would have stayed hidden had it not been for Gene's indiscretion.

I wondered what part Cliff Stone played in the real scenario. Since he was Ex-FBI, he would have known, or should have known, that Carlos Fawn was a wanted man. Maybe he had turned on the Feds after his arrest and conviction for murder in the drug bust. That was a possibility that I had to consider, but it wasn't really important at this point in my investigation, so I made a small note on the tablet:

"Check out Cliff Stone's connections."

I was there for quite some time. When I finished, I thought I had listed everything pretty much the way it happened and the connections from one event to the other.

1. Both Charles DuPont and Carlos Fawn had risen to high positions within the Mafia.

2. The New York mob wanted to take over the Florida operation, particularly the lottery.

3. Harry Fawn was a brilliant computer programmer who had control over the outcome of the lottery.

4. The New York family tried to convince Harry that he should abandon the Florida group and join forces with them.

5. The New York mob, through Sarcosi, had already determined that they were going to take over the lotto, regardless of Harry's decision, so they fixed the radio controlled fuel shut off valve prior to Harry's trip. Carlos was willing to negotiate so he sent Harry to New York.

6. Carlos's sources told him that the New York boys were going to kill Harry. He had ValJean Dupont rig a second transmitter that would blow up whomever attempted to activate the fuel shut off valve. Morgan got word of that and informed Charles DuPont. He

makes sure that the trigger man has the right transmitter.

7. Harriet Fawn had gone to New York for a shopping trip and was not expected to fly back with Harry. The last minute change in plans was not known to her father, Charles DuPont. He ordered Sarcosi to blow up the plane.

8. ValJean knew of the fuel shut off valve, the wreck, and the second transmitter. He puts the pieces in a rental place as his security and attempts a blackmail. The attempt fails. Fawn saws off one of his legs. ValJean had taken over the programming tasks after Harry's death and decides to fix the computer so that neither the New York mafia or the Florida mafia would benefit from the winning ticket. He programmed Mona the winning ticket, intending to cash it and disappear. Mona gets killed while delivering the ticket by an overzealous, drugged up Sarcosi, Jr.

9. ValJean goes into hiding, knowing that both sides of the 'gang' are looking for him, both sides will probably want him dead.

10. Carlos Fawn sends Cliff Stone and Gene to find ValJean, he wants the lotto ticket.

11. Charles DuPont hires Morgan to find ValJean.

12. DuPont hires me to find the killer for two reasons.

    1. He thinks the killer will have the lotto ticket.

    2. He wants proof of the second transmitter, and the man who caused his daughter and her husband to fall out of the sky.

13. Carlos Fawn realizes after my visit that things are getting hot for him and puts out a contract on me. I didn't realize what was going on until I get GiGi, then it dawns on me that Carlos might be wanting me dead.

After I had all of my thoughts outlined on the tablet, I made copies of my notes, put them in an envelope and mailed them to my home office back in Santa Monica, CA.

I had enough to start a FBI investigation into the lottery debacle, since the Florida lotto was sold in adjoining states, that made it a Federal Crime. I sent copies of my notes to the local FBI office.

I made a third set of copies of my notes and mailed them to Happs. Now with all my bases covered except one, I decided it was time to have my showdown with Sarcosi.

It would require some thinking. I'm not so stupid that I am going to march right in to the Lion's Den like Shell Scott did in some of Richard S. Prather's books. I'm not that dumb. This needed a plan that would be as devious as Shell Scott, as merciless as Mike Hammer, and as clever as Travis McGee.

I thought about it for a long time. I would need some help from my pilot friend, Spencer Adams.

If Sarcosi was as stupid as he had been when we pulled the dihydrogen monoxide gag, he would fall for it hook line and sinker.

I got on one of the computers in the library and typed a letter. I dated it three days before the newspaper article announcing ValJean DuPont's demise. I was thinking by the time Sarcosi gets the letter he'll think ValJean wrote it before he died.

Alfredo Sarcosi
c/o Sarcosi Deli
577 South Dixie Highway
Homestead, FL

Al

I don't want anymore fighting between us. I'm too old and too tired to worry about your goons beating me up. Here's the deal:

I've rigged a fuel shut off valve like the one I made for Harry Fawn's plane, and installed it on a plane owned by a guy named Spencer Adams.

I have information that a guy named Yardley has been giving you a bad time, and that you want him. Adams will be flying the airplane a week from Friday, Yardley will be with him. They are testing a water ski landing system that I built for Adams, so they can land on Coot's Bay.

The transmitter is in a rental place, Acme Rentals, in Atlanta. The space number is A3935 and it's in my name. You shouldn't have any trouble getting in, a padlock is all that is on it. Why am I doing this? Lets just say that if you find that lotto ticket you will share a little with me. Things have been bad for me and I could use the money.

Friends?

ValJean Dupont.

Now all I had to do was get to Atlanta, make sure that Sarcosi got the right transmitter and then get Spencer Adams to fly me out to Coot's Bay at 3 p.m. on Friday. If my hunch was right Sarcosi would send his kid to make Spencer Adams airplane with me in it, fall into the Everglades.

CHAPTER FORTY SEVEN

I took a six a.m. flight out of
Miami to Atlanta, arrived at 7:03. I
rented a car and took two hours to find
the Acme Rental space. It was a huge
complex with over a thousand spaces,
some as big as small aircraft hangars.

I found the office and talked to
the same clerk I had talked to on the
phone when I first called. She was
friendly and I turned on all of the
charm I could muster.

"Would you object to letting me
in that space? I won't take anything
out, you can watch me. I just want to
make sure that something that is
supposed to be there is actually there."

I showed her the folder with the
information I had, the one given to me
by Charles DuPont.

"Well, Mr. Yardley," she said in
a drawl, "I've got a few minutes. I can
walk over there with you. This is
highly unusual, without the owner's

permission, but I guess it'll be all right."

"The owner won't care," I said. "He's dead."

"Dead?"

"Yes, dead. I'm investigating his murder."

"Investigating?"

I opened my wallet and flipped my P.I. badge. She glanced at it, smiled and said something like they didn't have anything to hide, so it will be OK.

We left her office and walked twice the length of a football field to the rental space A3935. She opened one of the two padlocks needed to get in. The door was set so that the rental owner or the renter could open their respective lock and the door would open.

The door slid up and I looked inside. Most of the space was occupied by mangled sheet metal and broken glass, what was left of Harry Fawn's airplane. On the right of the space was a metal rack with three shelves. On the middle shelf was a cardboard box with black lettering "transmitter". Next to the box was the cylindrical object that I knew was the fuel shut off valve. I opened the box. There were identical transmitters inside, like garage door openers

One would blow me and the space and the clerk into the next world. The other one had, at one time, actuated a fuel shut off valve that killed a young man and a young woman.

I picked up the first one carefully and examined it. It had a single screw in the back that held together the two plastic halves. I took my pocket knife and unscrewed it carefully, laid the screw on the shelf and gingerly lifted the back half off the transmitter. It came apart easily and I stood with half of it in each hand. I turned first the left hand, then the right and looked inside. The one on the left had a circuit board with a bunch of resistors, capacitors and electrical stuff. The right hand one was the bottom part and inside I saw a glob of gray clay that looked like silly putty. C4 explosives.

It had been many years and I had no way of knowing if the battery was still good, so I had stopped at a hardware store and bought a pack of AA batteries, a pack of C size and a pack of two 9 volt batteries. It was a 9 volt that operated the transmitter. The battery hadn't leaked, deteriorated or rusted but I wanted to make sure it worked so I carefully pulled the harness off of it and replaced it. I put the two halves back together and put the screw back in it carefully.

"Find what you're looking for, honey?" The clerk said.

I glanced at her. She was about 40, not bad looking, dark hair and dark brown eyes. Her face had the wrinkles of a heavy smoker and a rasp in her voice told me that she had been rode hard and put away wet.

"I think so," I said. "I'd better check the other one though."

"OK." She said. "Take your time. I've got about twenty minutes. That should be time enough for whatever you want."

I ignored the implication and replaced the C4 transmitter in the box and took the other one. It opened the same way. Convinced that it was the one used to activate the fuel shut off valve I turned my back on the clerk and shoved it down in my pants, pulling my shirt down over it.

I turned and walked past her quickly.

"Is that all you want to see?" she asked slowly.

"Yes," I said.

"You sure? I've got plenty of time."

"What time do you get off?" I asked.

"Five," she said, smiling. "Then I'll have all the time you want."

"I'll call you," I said.

She frowned.

"I'm a little rushed for time, now, but I'll be back."

That seemed to satisfy her and I walked back with her to the office, took a twenty from my wallet and gave it to her.

"Oh that's not necessary," she said.

"Take it," I said. "You've gone out of your way to help me. Please, take it. And if someone else comes here to get in that space, let them in, but don't tell them I've been here. OK?"

She took it with a smile. "OK."

By the time she got off work I was back in Miami.

CHAPTER FORTY EIGHT

I addressed an envelope and put the phony letter in it and dropped it in Sarcosi's mailbox. A quarter, pushed into an ink pad and pressed over the stamp, made it look like a cancelled stamp. I had to hope that he would fall for it, but then if he didn't there were other ways to skin a cat. Or kill a rat.

It was Wednesday.

I waited three hours then called on Charles DuPont.

I kept my straight face on, never once letting on that I knew his real identity. In reporting to him, I gave him all of my activities except those that would lead him to believe that I was on to him. There is a time and a place for everything, and this wasn't the time to confront Charles DuPont.

"So you are convinced that it was Sarcosi who killed my daughter and her husband?"

"Yes," I said. "Everything I've learned leads me to that conclusion.

ValJean DuPont, on his death bed, gave me all the information regarding the fuel shut off valve, that it was Sarcosi who ordered it built. I got the rest from Carlos Fawn."

I was expecting it when Juan came to the study and announced that Mr. DuPont was wanted on the phone. I had a feeling that I knew who it was. Right on time.

"I'll take it in my office, Juan," he said.

When he returned he had a smile on his face. He looked like the Cheshire cat.

"You've done a good job, Yardley," he said. "I'm convinced that you are right. It seems that I owe you some money. Please come back on Friday evening around 6 p.m. and have dinner with me. I'll have your check ready for you."

"That sounds like a winner to me," I said, standing.

I shook hands with him and left.

Thursday I laid low. I got up early, took the Austin Healey and drove down to the Keys. I'd always had a yearning to visit the bar where Hemingway downed his booze. Sloppy Joe's is on Duval Street in the heart of Key West. Four foot tall neon letters across the front will tell you that you've found it.

The food there is good and the atmosphere typical Conch. There was a noon day entertainer, an unknown comedian who should have been on Leno.

"How many Conch's does it take to eat a possum?" he asked.

No one ventured an answer.

"Two," he announced solemnly. "One to eat the possum and one to watch for cars."

I thought it was hilarious. You could look around and tell who the regulars were. they weren't laughing. Tourists were splitting a gut.

By 10 p.m. I'd had a few too many rum drinks and found a room close by that cost more than the Madonna Inn in California. Three times the rate I was paying in Miami. I slept off the drinks, woke refreshed and ready for Friday. I showered, had breakfast at a local coffee shop and headed north for my meeting with Spencer Adams and our flight down to Coot's Bay.

CHAPTER FORTY NINE

Spencer Adams hadn't asked any questions when I asked him to fly me down to Coot's Bay.

Now, however, when I told him what my plan consisted of, he had reservations.

"You just don't seem like the kind of man that would intentionally kill someone."

"I've killed before, but only in self defense," I told him. "And when you look at it from my point of view, you'll see that this is self defense."

"More like vigilante justice to me," he growled, I could hear the displeasure through the headphones. "I wish you had let me know. I'm not pleased with taking part in vigilante justice."

"Just let me have my say, Spence," I said. "If I can't convince you in two or three minutes, you can turn this plane around and fly back to Coral Gables. First, as a former law enforcement officer, you know how many criminals never serve time, never get their just rewards. I've already told you about this case, that the Mafia has control in high places here in Florida."

"If I just turn all of this over to the authorities, what are the odds that Sarcosi's kid will ever go to the pen, let alone get the death penalty? He's already killed one person and got off because the mob threatened the prosecuting attorney. People run scared all the time. He'd never be arrested, probably, unless Happs hauled him in. Then he'd be out on bond and either disappear or never come to trial."

I paused for a second and looked at him. I could see by the look on his face that he realized I was right.

"He's just a kid," he said. "If he is put in jail, he may change his ways. That's what our judicial system is all about, giving someone a second chance."

"You're right," I said, acknowledging the truth of his

statement. "But we both know that this kid will never change."

"Even Madam Justice Sotomayor believes that some people are just plain evil and he's a carbon copy of his old man. He's Mafia minded. He wants the power, the money and the prestige. He enjoys pushing people around. He enjoyed cutting Mona's throat and watching her life's blood spurt out on the sand."

"I've thought this thing out," I said. "He will push that button with the full intent to kill both you and me. He will be thinking that he'll get another feather in his cap, another way to make his bones to gain favor with the Capo."

The nose of the plane kept in a straight line following the highway towards Buttonwood Canal. If he intended to turn the plane around, Adams gave no sign of it. I could only talk to him over the closed circuit microphone and headsets on board the plane, but I was sure I was getting through to him.

"So this isn't a vengeful thing your doing, then?"

"No." I said. "I don't get any kick out of this kind of revenge. The stunt you and I pulled on Sarcosi was my idea of revenge. This is justice, to me."

"OK, Kip." He finally said.

"No regrets?"

"No regrets" he said. "I understand your point of view, and you summed it up when you said that he thinks you and I would both die if he had the right transmitter."

"Exactly," I said.

We had reached a point out over the Everglades when I thought the trigger man would be waiting below. We were flying at just over a thousand feet and I could see cars below us down on highway 9336.

One in particular caught my attention. It was GiGi's car. I knew that GiGi was still cooling his heels in Happs jailhouse. I picked up a pair of binoculars and focused on the car. It didn't surprise me to see Al Sarcosi, Jr.

driving. He was laughing and having a big time. I told Adams to look below.

I looked ahead of the Caddy down the narrow highway, trying to pick a spot where he would turn off and wait for the Piper Cub to fly over. Al Sarcosi, Jr. would then pick up the transmitter and laugh and push the button.

There was a road that went to the right off of 9336, maybe three miles in front of the Cadillac. That would be the spot, I thought, and a good one. There was little traffic on 9336 and none on the side road. I watched as the beautiful car slowed and turned off the highway. A hundred yards or so onto the side road it pulled to the right and stopped.

I was watching through the binoculars as Sarcosi reached in the glove compartment and pulled out the transmitter. He pointed it up at the airplane, a broad grin on his pock-marked face.

A balloon of fire appeared where the Cadillac had been. The sound didn't get to the Piper until after the shock wave had bounced the small plane.

"It's done," I said. "Let's go home."

Adams pushed the controls forward a little, tilted the aircraft's wing slightly and we made a smooth, controlled turn back to the East and headed back to Coral Gables.

CHAPTER FIFTY

I tied the dome raft up at the spot in the marina where ValJean DuPont had resided the day I met him. Spencer Adams had taken me to Coot's Bay and I took along enough gasoline to power the nine horsepower Honda motor pushing the raft down Buttonwood Canal and around Florida Bay back to the marina.

The young marina attendant came out to meet me and I threw him the line. He pulled the raft up tight to the wharf and handed me the line as I stepped ashore.

"I sure was sorry to hear about Mr. DuPont," he said.

"Yeah," I said, and let it go at that.

There was a reason I had brought the raft back and I wanted to get on with it. I would need a few things to finish that part of my plan, and I called a cab. I had the cab driver stop at a pawn shop and bought a twelve gauge shotgun, the same model that ValJean had been holding the day we found him near death. If my hunch was correct, it would suit the purpose fine.

I had bribed a service station near my motel room to let me keep the Austin Healey locked up in their service bay at night and it had been there for two days. I wanted to make sure they hadn't left it out while I was on the raft.

I gave the attendant a fifty and he assured me that they had locked it up every night during my absence. To be on the safe side, however, I popped the hood and looked everything over very carefully. I had the mechanic put it up on the rack and inspected the underside, looking for anything suspicious. It all seemed in order. I just wanted to make sure.

I spotted a blue Ford sedan down the block and across the street from the motel. It was there when I got out of the cab and it was still there while I inspected the Austin Healey. I figured it would pull away from the curb a block or so behind me when I left, and I was right.

By this time I was pretty sure that Sarcosi would come for me personally. I didn't think he'd send his hoods, plant explosives, or create an accident. I thought I knew enough about him now to know that he would want to watch me die. He would take his time, find me alone, and he would come for me.

I had paid the pawn shop guy a lot of extra money to skip the waiting period and as I drove back to the marina I was thinking how gun laws are worthless. Criminals or anyone with the right connections or money, can get a gun any time, just as I had done.

It took me less than twenty minutes to complete my task. I sat at the small table in ValJean DuPont's raft and read a book that he had left on his unmade bunk. It was Spillane's "Vengeance is Mine." Very fitting, I thought.

The bright Florida sun was sitting to the west, the shadow of the dome stretched out over the wooden dock. I could see out the small window of the door. The quiet hum of ValJean's air conditioner, and the gentle lapping of water on the back edge of the raft were the only sounds I could hear. Soon the sun would sink below the sea and twilight would envelope the marina. It wouldn't be long now, I was sure of it.

An hour after dark I was deeply engrossed in the book but became keenly aware instantly of the heavy footsteps coming towards the raft across the dock. I waited.

There was just one man, a heavy man from the sound of the footprints. They got louder as they got closer. The person who was coming was making no attempt to soften his footfalls. It was as though he wanted me to know that he was coming. I had turned on a small reading light behind me, and I knew that I was silhouetted dangerously.

The door wasn't locked. The knob turned, not slowly, not fast, it just turned. The door swung open. Sarcosi stepped in, closed the door behind him and stood looking at me. He had a .45 in his hand. His eyes were hollow looking and his face was gaunt.

"You killed my boy," he said, softly.

"Your boy killed himself," I said.

"Don't get fancy with words," he hissed. "I'm going to kill you, you schmuck. I tried to tell you to back off. You wouldn't listen. Now you're a dead man."

"Which do you want more, Sarcosi? Me dead or the lotto ticket?"

The gun in his hand waved slightly, very slightly. A gleam appeared in his eyes. I knew I had his attention.

"Have a seat," I said and shoved the chair opposite me away from the table with my foot.

"You've got the ticket?" He asked.

"Lets talk," I said. I laid the book down, took off my reading glasses and laid them on the table. "You haven't answered my question. Do you want the ticket more than you want me dead?"

"You're a dead man, Yardley," he said. "I've got ways that will make you puke that ticket. You're treading on ground that you have no idea about."

"Like you made ValJean talk?" I said. "A chain saw, chewing off his leg? Sit down, Sarcosi. You have to know me by now. I'm not afraid of your mad dog tactics. You don't scare me worth a crap."

He pulled the chair back and eased himself into it, the .45 still pointed at my chest.

"OK" He said. "Have it your way, schmuck. I don't care about the ticket. If it's never cashed that suits my purpose just as well. But I'm willing to listen. What have you got besides the ticket?"

"I've got it all, Sarcosi," I said. "I know the entire story. I know names, places, details that you wish were hidden forever. I can put you in jail for a hundred years with what I know. You know that, don't you?"

"I know one damned thing, schmuck. You killed my boy. You

messed in places where you shouldn't have. I kill you and no-one goes to jail. You should know that if you know the rest."

My right hand lowered carefully to my lap and I felt for the ring on the edge of the table. When I had it, I prodded him a little harder.

"You're just like you're kid," I said. "You're a punk. You send little boys to do a man's job. You hire goons to do your dirty work. You wouldn't make a pimple on a good Capo's ass."

"Die, schmuck!" He said, and raised the gun slightly, extended it towards me.

A split second more and I would be history. I pulled the ring.

The twelve gage roared its lethal voice. The impact sent the chair and its occupant sliding back two feet away from the table. Sarcosi sat there with a hole the size of a large saucer in this chest.

CHAPTER FIFTY ONE

Now it was time to confront Charles DuPont. I dreaded it. He was Tami's great grandfather. I had killed her other great grandfather by slicing open his chest with a chain saw. Now I was all set to do whatever I had to do.

Juan answered me on the intercom, checked with the boss man, and let me in. Charles was pleasant enough when he greeted me. I didn't know what to expect, but pleasantry wasn't high on my list.

"Come in, Kip," he said, smiling.

"Good morning, Charles," I said.

"I heard about Al Sarcosi," he told me, but the smile was still there.

"Senior or Junior?"

"Both," he said. "Good riddance of bad rubbish, in my humble opinion."

"Really now?" I asked, knowing that my eyebrows had lifted when I said it.

"What's on your mind, Kip?"

"Well, I figured it different," I said. "I thought that you and the Sarcosi family were good friends. It took me aback when you said they were bad rubbish."

"I knew Sarcosi," he said. "We were never friends."

"Even when you were part of the New York mafia?" I asked, putting my hole card face up on the table.

He looked at me for a long time, his eyes never wavering from my face.

"I see," he said, finally. "You know about me?"

"Yes."

"Well there are things you probably do not know," he said. "I quit the mafia. I'm probably one of maybe two or three former Dons who quit and lived to tell it."

"You quit?"

"Yes." He turned towards the door and motioned to Juan. "Bring me a bottle of good wine, Juan. Mr. Yardley and I have to talk."

I listened.

"I quit before the big fight between Al Sarcosi and Charlie Cervato. Sarcosi wanted to be the Godfather here in Florida and I had no objection to that, I just wanted out. I met with some people and told them my plans, they agreed to them, and I quit. Simple as that."

"I've heard that no one quits," I said. "Too much information floating around. Too many skeletons in too many closets."

"One thing that you have to know about me," he said, holding up his hand as if to say 'stop', "I never killed a man, and never ordered a hit on anyone. All of the power that I gained through the ranks was by my wits, not my fists."

"Meaning?"

"I mean that I used my head, Kip," he said. "I started investing in legitimate businesses on behalf of my constituents."

"Constituents?" I laughed out loud. "That term is used by congressmen and senators, it's funny to hear it coming from a Capo."

"Please don't use that term, Kip," he said. "It's never appealed to me. I preferred 'consigliore' then and still do. You see, I wanted a different life for my daughter and my

grandchildren. I still would like that.
I'm willing to pay you not to reveal any
of this to Tami. She doesn't have to
know. Name your price, Kip, and I'll
write you a check."

"The money you said you'd pay
for finding out the truth about your
daughter's death and the name of the
scum who killed Mona. That's all the
money I want."

"You won't tell Tami?"

"I don't know why I should. I
have one question, though."

"Ask."

"No one ever told you that your
daughter died because she chose to fly
back to Miami with Harry rather than
take the commercial flight she had
booked?"

"Oh, I knew that," he said. "She
called me that evening and told me.
She and Harry had quarreled about
him flying his plane to New York, she
didn't like small planes, and it upset
her when he bought his. They argued
about it all the time. When she called I
told her that if she loved him she would
try to understand his wants, not fight

them. She said that she would try. I
suggested that she fly back with him."

"So you knew nothing about the
fuel shut off valve until Morgan told
you?"

"Nothing," he repeated. "I
hadn't kept up with the struggle for
control in the family. As far as I was
concerned, family had an entirely
different meaning."

"What about the phone call from
Sarcosi the last time I was here?" I
asked. "I was thinking that he told you
about what I had discovered, you had
him send his kid to punch my button."

"I didn't get a call from Sarcosi,"
he said, looking puzzled. "What call?"

"Juan came and told you that
you had a phone call. You said, "I'll
take it in the study." Wasn't that call
from Sarcosi?"

"No." He said. "That call was
from my broker. I told you I invested
in legal things. I own stock in several
banks here in Miami, and he was
advising me about some holdings that
were in jeopardy because the FBI had
found connections to the underground.

It seems they got a folder from you that detailed a lot of what you have told me."

"Oh," I said. My mind was racing back to that day. I realized that I had made a false assumption. At that time I thought that Charles DuPont was still calling the shots. Now that I thought about it, if he had ordered the hit on Harry Fawn and knew that Harriet was going to be on that plane, he would have cancelled it. It was all falling in place now.

"Is something wrong, Kip?"

"No." I said. "I'm just remembering what a friend told me recently."

"What's that?" he asked.

"He said that people can change if given the time and opportunity."

"I changed, Kip," he said, looking me straight in the eye. "I gave it up. Even my spiritual life changed. I've been going to St. Peters here in Miami since the day I quit the mob. I've donated thousands to local charities. God has changed my life."

"I believe he has," I said. I finished my wine and sat the glass on the table.

He rose and excused himself, and left the room.

There had been so many twists and turns to this case that I half expected him to return with a Thompson Sub-machine gun pointed at me. Instead he returned with a check for a hundred thousand dollars.

CHAPTER FIFTY TWO

The Austin Healey engine sounded sweet to my ears as I left Charles DuPont's estate and headed back to my motel room. I felt good, satisfied that I had given the case every thing that I could. It was now time to go see Tami and decide what I was going to do with the rest of my life.

By the time I got near my motel it had started to warm up considerably and I had the top up on the Healey. I glanced down at the dash, found the button I wanted and turned it on. Cool air from the aftermarket air conditioner surged into the cockpit and felt good.

Air conditioner.

Something buzzed in my brain. I felt like there was an electrical connection from my brain to the air conditioner. A buzzing sound. At first I thought the unit was making a noise. Then slowly, like gradually turning up the speed on a variable speed phonograph player, I realized that the noise was in my head.

Air conditioner.

Those two words repeated in my mind. Then repeated again, and again.

Air conditioner. Air conditioner. Air conditioner.

I concentrated for a few minutes, focusing. Then suddenly I knew.

I made a U-turn and headed the Healey back towards Homestead, pushing the accelerator down until the needle on the speedometer hit sixty, fifteen miles per hour over the speed limit. I'd risk it. I had to know.

When I hit NE 8th St I made a left so fast that the new Michelins squealed on the blacktop. They squealed again when I made a quick right on NE 43rd Avenue and a final left on to SW 328th. By then I could smell the heat of the tires. I opened it up and flipped the electric overdrive switch.

A flash of thought went through my mind. The electric overdrive was one place I hadn't inspected the day that I checked the Healey for explosives before I drove back to the Marina. Now I was hitting seventy eight on the narrow blacktop road, headed towards the same Marina.

Its funny how thoughts like that will pop into your head but when it did I took my right hand off of the switch and put it firmly back on the wheel and stared straight ahead of me.

I roared into the Marina parking lot and hit the brakes, spinning the wheel and sliding the Healey into a slot near where the domed raft sat gently rising and falling in the water. The young attendant jumped out of his chair and looked at me puzzled as I opened the door and ran towards the raft.

Yellow "CRIME SCENE, DO NOT CROSS" tape was still around the raft. No one was in sight so I ignored the tape and flipped the door open. Sarcosi's body had long since been removed but the brown blood stain was still on the door, along with pieces of rotting flesh.

I ignored them.

My heart was beating like a whisk would beat eggs for an omelet. It had to be here. It *had to be!*

"You almost bought it from me for forty bucks." I could hear ValJean saying, almost as if he were standing there in front of me.

"I've got to buy some wire to fix this air conditioner and I won't get my check until next week."

I opened the panel on the front of the air conditioner. There were a bunch of wires inside. I pushed them gently aside, looking behind them.

Nothing.

I paused momentarily and scratched my head. Then I saw the label on the inside of the panel. It was lose at the top. I gripped the top between thumb and forefinger on my left hand and pulled down gently.

There behind the label was the Florida Power Vault lotto ticket worth one hundred and fourteen million dollars.

CHAPTER FIFTY THREE

Tami cried when I gave her the ticket. She started with just a gasp, then a slight sniffle, then deep sobbing moans, tears flowing faster than a sudden summer shower. I stood there with my arms around her waist, waiting.

After a long time she gently pushed me away and walked into the kitchen of the home she had lived in all of her life. I stood there thinking of everything that had transpired since the day I had met her on the beach. My feelings were starting to creep up on me.

I had killed two men. If you want to call two blood thirsty, money-crazed, Mafioso minded hoodlums men. Nevertheless, they were human beings, living, breathing, just as I lived and breathed. They had families, just as I had a family.

But that's where the similarity ended. I knew that God, in his infinite wisdom, would forgive me. All I had to do was ask. And I did. As I stood there listening to Tami sobbing softly in the kitchen, I bowed my head and said in my mind, "God forgive me."

"Kip?"

I heard her tiny voice. I walked into the kitchen. She was standing there with the lotto ticket in her right hand, her left hand on the knob of the old cook stove where Mona had cooked the best meal of my life.

"Yes?" I said.

She turned the knob. The pilot light on the stove gave a little click and the burner answered with a whoosh. Her right hand extended, slowly. She touched the lotto ticket to the flame and it immediately caught on fire. She carried it to the kitchen sink and held it until it burned her fingers, then dropped it into the sink and stood watching it curl into a blackened ash.

I watched silently. It was her ticket, she had the choice. I think she made the right one.

THE END.

Don Yarber lives with his wife, Shirley, near Morganfield, KY. He is currently writing on his first Western Novel, "Train to the Sun":

Will's body lay heavy in the saddle in front of me. He was still alive, although he shouldn't be. His breathing had almost stopped and when I put my ear to his chest I could barely hear his heart beat. I had ridden fifty miles with him across the saddle, me sitting behind the cantle, pushing the gelded paint as hard as I dared.